The
❧ Panchatantra ❧

Narindar Uberoi Kelly was born in Lahore, then British India. Educated at Punjab and Lucknow Universities, she went to England, and then on to the United States, where she received a PhD in South Asia Regional Studies at the University of Pennsylvania, focusing on social demography, an experience that provided her a richer understanding of the sociocultural traditions of India. Her professional career has been that of a social demographer working in the fields of health, education and finance. She lives in Baltimore, USA, with her husband, Michael Kelly.

Meagan Jenigen is a 2013 graduate of the Maryland Institute College of Art. In addition to exhibiting drawings, paintings and illustrations, she works in apparel and theatre design, as well as video production and documentaries. She is a native of Richmond, VA, USA.

The Panchatantra

TEACHING TALES OF OLD INDIA

Retold by
Narindar Uberoi Kelly

Illustrations by
Meagan Jenigen

hachette
INDIA

First published in five volumes in 2014 by Trafford Publishing, USA

This single-volume edition first published in 2017 by Hachette India
(Registered name: Hachette Book Publishing India Pvt. Ltd)
An Hachette UK company
www.hachetteindia.com

1

ISBN: 978-93-5195-129-2

Hachette Book Publishing India Pvt. Ltd
4th & 5th Floors, Corporate Centre
Plot No. 94, Sector 44, Gurgaon 122003, India

Typeset in Minion Pro 12/16 by
Manmohan Kumar, New Delhi

Printed and bound in India
by Replika Press Pvt. Ltd.

For my family,
who light up my life:
My love Michael Kelly;
My daughter Kieran, her husband Ian Holmes,
their son, Jandiga;
My son Sean, his wife Olivia Ma, their
daughters, Aurora and Christina

Advisory: This edition follows the original *Panchatantra*, and consequently a few of the themes in some of the stories in this edition may not be appropriate for young children, or may express attitudes towards women that were prevalent in those times. Parents and teachers can help young readers understand these issues.

Contents

Note to the Reader

I fell in love with the *Panchatantra* stories as a tween who stumbled across them in a library at a time when my family were refugees as a result of the Partition of India between what is now Pakistan and India. I suppose part of the attraction of the stories was to get away from the realities of being homeless in a part of India that seemed a different country, with people speaking different languages and eating food quite unlike anything I was used to. But the stories helped me by giving me some insight into what and why my parents were trying to teach me – and some appreciation for what I was resisting in a world turned upside down by our narrow escape from the violence and turmoil of our loss of home and country.

I decided I wanted my grandchildren to have access to these stories that meant so much to me, but in a language that they could easily understand. As I adapted the stories for modern readers, it occurred to me that one of the great strengths of the *Panchatantra* (literally 'the five books') derives from what at first seems the sheer nonsense of listening in to animals talking like humans. Yet this absurd conceit of animals chatting and arguing and telling stories immediately establishes a strangely safe distance between the reader and these creatures. And even more strangely, we are transformed into observers and compatriots in their struggles with thorny issues of friendship, collaboration, conflict and ambition. If I was particularly taken with these tales at a time of vulnerability and uncertainty in my life, readers approaching and experiencing adolescence and young maturity (when does that process end?) are in some sense similarly adrift and puzzled by the unfamiliar new land of adulthood. Readers of these tales are assumed to be much like I was – expatriates operating in a new landscape they don't fully understand.

The genius of these stories is their relentless unwillingness to whitewash or romanticize life. They depict the ignoble as well as the noble, cruelty and deceit as well as honour, foolishness as much as cunning, deception as rampant as honesty. They show the underside as well as glimpses of fulfillment in life. The stories unveil the contradictory nature of life, its tensions, risks and dangers as well as its rewards. And it accomplishes this through the disorienting welter of stories within stories that pile up on each other to convey a kind of confusion that forms a powerful antidote to other literary forms designed to convey wisdom – like preaching, teaching, or telling people what to do. Out of this turmoil, somehow wisdom can emerge as a deeper appreciation of the dangers, tensions and value of leading a good life.

A word of caution: some of these stories illustrate Indian practices of many centuries past. Women are not often depicted or treated well, a phenomenon that continues to this day. But the stories have much to tell us. I trust that parents will help their children to understand the age-old realities described in this book and use the occasion to teach their own values.

Narindar Uberoi Kelly

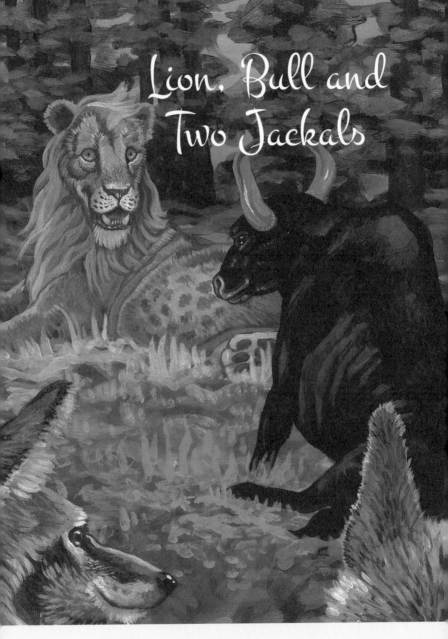

Lion, Bull and Two Jackals

Book One

About this Book

Book One, here titled simply 'Lion, Bull and Two Jackals', deals with friendship. It shows how the close friendship between the Lion and the Bull was formed, grew and eventually was destroyed by a mean and conniving Jackal. It highlights how friendships, indeed all relationships, need tending. Cultivating a friendship, like cultivating a flower, needs careful nurturing, feeding and pruning. But the lessons go beyond how to treasure and keep enduring friendships. They include how to treat others with respect, honesty and loyalty, and how to judge when others are trying to do you harm.

In the *frame* story, Crafty, an unemployed jackal, looking to win favour with the Lion who rules his forest, introduces the Lion to the Bull. When the Lion and the Bull become close friends, Crafty seeks to destroy the friendship. Cautious, another unemployed jackal, tries to stop Crafty from doing the unforgivable. In the end Crafty succeeds and the Lion kills the Bull.

Inside the frame story are 33 *nesting* stories. One set are stories that Crafty tells the Lion and Bull to promote himself. Another set are stories the Bull tells Crafty to smooth things over when he himself is obviously in danger (but he is telling them to the wrong animal). Most of the stories form the debate between the two jackals: Cautious tells stories to prevent Crafty from destroying the friendship between the Lion and the Bull, or Crafty tells stories to Cautious to justify his actions. The remaining stories are deeper nesting stories. Three stories are connected because one character appears in all of them. Two are connected because the storyteller is the same. A group of five stories illustrate a David and Goliath situation, and involve ways the weak can prevail but only with the aid of friends.

Each story, or group of stories, is separated into the frame story of the Lion, Bull and two Jackals, and the *stand-alone* or nesting stories that illustrate the lessons of the frame story. The frame story presents the do's and don'ts of life and is told on the coloured pages while the stand-alone stories in coloured text on white pages illustrate the point or lesson articulated in the frame story. This arrangement helps the reader to choose to read or ignore the frame stories that deal with life lessons. The frame story can be read without interruption of the illustrating stories. The book can be read in its entirety to experience the original design of this book of stories.

Lion, Bull and Two Jackals

Stories	Told By	To
• Wedge-pulling Monkey	Cautious, Jackal	Crafty, Jackal
• Jackal and the War Drum	Crafty, Jackal	Rusty, Lion
• Merchant Named Able	Crafty, Jackal	Lively, Bull
• Pious and Cheat	Crafty, Jackal	Cautious, Jackal
• Jackal at the Ram Fight	Crafty, Jackal	Cautious, Jackal
• Weaver's Wife	Crafty, Jackal	Cautious, Jackal
• Crow-Hen and the Black Snake	Crafty, Jackal	Cautious, Jackal
• Heron Who Liked Crabmeat	A Jackal	A Crow
• Arrogant and Rabbit	Crafty, Jackal	Cautious, Jackal
• Weaver Who Loved a Princess	Crafty, Jackal	Cautious, Jackal
• Grateful Animals and Ungrateful Man	Crafty, Jackal	Rusty, Lion
• Leap and Creep	Crafty, Jackal	Rusty, Lion
• Blue Jackal	Lively, Bull	Crafty, Jackal
• Swan and Owl	Lively, Bull	Crafty, Jackal

- Gullible Camel — Lively, Bull — **Crafty, Jackal**
- Lion and Carpenter — Lively, Bull — **Crafty, Jackal**
- Sandpiper and the Sea — Crafty, Jackal — **Lively, Bull**
- Turtle and Two Ganders — Steady, Sandpiper — **Brag, Sandpiper**
- Forethought, Ready Wit and Fatalist — Steady, Sandpiper — **Brag, Sandpiper**
- Sparrow versus Elephant — Steady, Sandpiper — **Brag, Sandpiper**
- Clever Old Gander — Wise Old Bird — **Group of Birds**
- Lion and Ram — Old Bird — **Garuda, Bird-King**
- Jackal Who Tricked Lion — Crafty, Jackal — **Cautious, Jackal**
- Monk Who Left His Body Behind — Cautious, Jackal — **Crafty, Jackal**
- Girl Who Married a Snake — Sage, Counsellor — **Gold-Throne, King**
- Parrot Named Brilliant — The Girl — **Group of People**
- Unteachable Monkey — Cautious, Jackal — **Crafty, Jackal**
- Honest and Sly — Cautious, Jackal — **Crafty, Jackal**
- The Cure Was Worse than the Disease — Sly's Father — **Sly**
- Mice That Ate Iron — Cautious, Jackal — **Crafty, Jackal**
- Twin Parrots, Good and Bad — Cautious, Jackal — **Crafty, Jackal**
- Sensible Foe — Cautious, Jackal — **Crafty, Jackal**
- Foolish Friend — Cautious, Jackal — **Crafty, Jackal**

There was a king called Immortal-Power who lived in a fabulous city that had everything. He had three sons. They were truly ignorant. The King saw that they could not figure things out and did not want to learn. They hated school. So the King asked a very wise man to wake up their brains. The wise man, a Brahmin named Sharma, took the three Princes to his home. Every day he told them stories that taught the Princes lessons on how to live intelligently. To make sure they would never forget, he made them learn the stories by heart. The first set of teaching tales Sharma told was: **Lion, Bull and Two Jackals.**

Sharma began:

'The Lion and Bull
Were friends until
A Jackal intervened,
Who was wily and mean –
Then friendship died.'

'How come?' asked the three Princes, and Sharma told this story.

Lion, Bull and Two Jackals

There once was a very rich merchant who lived in a city in India called Sunrise. It was a great city – well laid out at the foot of tall mountains and very prosperous. The Merchant was content living there until it dawned on him that although he had lots of money he should try to make more of it by putting it to good use. After all, riches should be hard-earned, carefully protected, ever increased by savvy investing, and shared wisely. Money unused is money unpossessed.

So the merchant collected his merchandise wagon, hired some workers, harnessed his two lucky bulls named Joyful and Lively, and went forth towards a bigger city to make more money.

On the journey, the team had to go through a dense forest. When they were halfway through it, the bull named Lively snapped his yoke, fell and badly injured a leg. He could not go on further. So, with much regret, the Merchant ordered him to be left behind with some feed just in case the leg healed.

After a few weeks in the jungle, Lively did get better. He found plenty to eat and plenty to explore. He began to have a good time and made a lot of noise.

One day a lion named Rusty, with a big bushy golden mane, was passing nearby with his animal staff, servants and subjects. Rusty heard Lively bellow, and was both surprised and bothered. He had never heard such a sound before.

Now a Lion, King of the Jungle, has a company: the lion himself, his ministers and advisors, his attendants and guards, and his subjects, with each class divided into high, middle and low. Rusty was accepted as King by them all because of unbound pride, exceptional courage and incomparable self-esteem that brooked no rivals. Rusty was King because he behaved like a king: fearless, valiant, dignified, selfless, and without reproach, pretence and dependency. His deeds crowned him King.

Among Rusty's followers there were two jackals, sons of former ministers with some hereditary rights, but currently out of a job. Their names were Cautious and Crafty. When Crafty saw that Rusty seemed bothered by the bellows everyone had heard, he began to plot harm to Rusty. Cautious tried to stop him: 'Why meddle?' he said. 'Remember the wedge-pulling monkey.'

'Come again?' asked Crafty. So Cautious told this story. 🖉

Wedge-pulling Monkey

A wealthy merchant was having a temple built. Every afternoon the workers would take a break and go have lunch away from the site. One day, a troop of monkeys from a nearby park came by and began climbing all over the unfinished temple. It was such fun. One of them noticed a wedge put up by the workmen at the very top of the building frame to keep a huge log from rolling down. Without a thought, the curious monkey pulled the wedge to see what would happen.

Well, the big log rolled down and crushed him before he could get out of the way.

'That is why bright people avoid meddling,' said Cautious. 'We may not be employed by King Rusty, but we pick up enough to make do even as hangers-on.'

Crafty wasn't having it. 'We could be hired if we show good service and someone else could be fired if he is not deserving.'

'What are you implying?' asked Cautious.

'King Rusty is scared, and his servants are frightened and don't know what to do,' said Crafty.

'How do you know?' asked Cautious and Crafty replied, *Intelligent men can infer correctly from other people's body language what is going on.* I am a judge of occasion and know how to follow do's and don'ts like:

'Look for the right time to try persuading someone;
Be cautious;
Don't take what belongs to others;
Stay close to those in power;
Love the King's friends and hate his foes;
Serve only masters who have merit;
Invest only where there is profit;
Always be ready to flatter;
Above all, get to know your King.'

So Crafty went to meet Rusty and said, 'I know you do not need me right now, but I want to see if I can be of use to a master who is fair in his dealings. After all, the quality of the servant depends upon the use the master makes. I am only a jackal, but my worth is not in my birth; rather, it is told by my deeds.'

'Speak freely,' said Rusty.

'Why did you turn back when you heard a bellow?'

Rusty pondered: 'Even Kings find comfort in sharing their troubles with honest and faithful friends and servants. He seems trustworthy. I will tell him.'

'Some monstrous creature has come to my jungle,' Rusty replied. 'He is unknown, but his bellow must match his nature and power. He sounds dangerous, so I turned back.'

'What!' Crafty said. 'Frightened by a sound? The wise do not leave without making sure that the new place will be better than the old. Besides, there are many sounds that do not warn of danger. Remember how easily one can be fooled. Remember the jackal and the war drum.'

'What was that?' asked Rusty, and Crafty told this story.

Jackal and the War Drum

A hungry jackal was searching for food. He came upon a king's battleground in the middle of a forest and suddenly heard a loud sound. He got really scared, thinking: 'What kind of creature made that sound? It must be huge. I am dead.'

But keeping his wits, he started to cautiously, quietly, look around and saw a war drum. He did not know what it was. He noticed the sound came from it but only when a gust of wind swung a tree branch against it. The jackal got less and less scared and more and more curious.

'Maybe I can eat this creature and satisfy my hunger,' he thought, 'it is fat.' But the jackal was very surprised when he tried to take a mouthful. 'What a fool I am,' laughed the jackal. 'I thought it full of fat, so I crept in . . . to find nothing but old wood and dry skin.'

'However,' objected Rusty, 'my servants are too frightened to go explore the sound.'

'I will go and check,' said Crafty. 'Be brave until I return.'

When Crafty left, Rusty began to have second thoughts. 'I was too trusting to show fear to this jackal. *I should have remembered that the careful, even when weak, will be safe from the enemy, while the too trusting strong will fall quickly to the foe.*'

Meanwhile, Crafty had discovered the bull named Lively and gleefully started plotting to get Rusty in his power by suggesting war and peace with Lively.

Crafty went back to Rusty. 'Did you see the creature?' asked Rusty.

'Yes,' said Crafty, 'and with your permission, will bring him to you.'

Crafty then went to Lively. 'Our master, Rusty, wants to know why you are not afraid to do all this bellowing.'

'Who is Rusty?' asked Lively.

'What!' said Crafty. 'You do not even know our master Rusty? He is a mighty lion, King of the Jungle, with many ministers, servants and subjects, the proud lord of life and riches.'

When Lively heard this he thought: 'I am dead.' In despair, he asked Crafty for help: 'You seem nice, please ask your master to give me safe passage and I will leave.'

'You stay right here,' said Crafty. 'When Rusty agrees to this, I will come and take you to him.'

Crafty went back to Rusty and said, 'This creature has the blessings of the Great God Shiva to make this forest his playground.'

'What did you say to him?' asked Rusty.

'I told him – "This forest is the domain of Rusty, the mount of Great God Shiva's wife, so you are a guest,"' said Crafty. '"Come meet Rusty and make your home with him: eat, drink, work and play with him," to which Lively replied, "As long as you make your master grant me safe passage," and I answered, "That's up to the master."'

'I will grant him safe conduct, but Lively must take an oath of loyalty to me,' said Rusty.

Crafty thought: 'The master is gracious to me and ready to do what I say.'

So he went to Lively, gave the bull the good news, but also made him promise to always act in agreement with him as the counsellor from now on. With such an alliance both Crafty and Lively would enjoy King Rusty's favour.

'Remember, Lively, to always pay honour to a King's people,' said Crafty.

'In what way?' asked Lively, and Crafty told this story. 🍀

Merchant Named Able

There lived a merchant named Able who did all the city business where he lived and all the royal business too. He was very clever to be able to do this for it is hard to serve two masters, the city and the king, when things that have to be done are often contradictory.

When Able's daughter was to be married, the Merchant invited the citizens and everyone in the king's company, feasted them and gave them presents. When the wedding was over, he escorted the King and his ladies back to the palace, all the while showing great respect.

Now, the King had a house-cleaner named Bull who had once taken a seat that did not belong to him in the presence of dignitaries and Able had cuffed him and shown him the door. Bull had felt so humiliated that he could not get over it. But while the old insult still rankled, he also knew that he could do nothing.

Until one day when he was sweeping near where the King lay half-awake in his bed, he saw a chance to get even, so he said out loud, 'How awful it is, Able kissing the Queen!'

The King jumped up and wanted to know if Bull had spoken the truth. 'I had a bad night, Your Majesty, and do not remember what I said.' replied Bull. But the King was jealous and suspicious, remembering all the proverbs about unfaithful women. He promptly withdrew his favour from Able, who was very shocked for he had never done any unfriendly act against the King or anyone else.

One day, after some time had gone by, Bull insulted Able in public and, finally, Able put it all together. *He realized that servants get as upset as anyone else when shown disrespect in public.* Clearly Bull had nursed an old grudge and when he got a chance at payback, he took it. Able decided to make amends. He gave Bull a big gift and explained that Bull had made a mistake in public for which he had been cuffed and humiliated. Bull was thrilled with the present and the apology, and promised to make things right with the King.

The next day Bull went to the palace where the King was half-asleep and said in a loud voice: 'Gee! When the King is on the toilet, he eats cucumbers.'

'What!' shouted the King 'How dare you!'

'Oh, King, I had a bad night and know not what I say,' answered Bull.

The King realized that Bull's earlier comment about Able too must have been untrue and gave the merchant his honours back.

Lively got the point of the story and agreed to the alliance that Crafty wanted. Together they went to Rusty's camp and Crafty introduced Lively, who bowed low to the King. Rusty extended his paw and was respectful in return.

Rusty asked Lively why he lived in the forest and Lively told him how he came to be there. Rusty promised to allow Lively to live his own life in the forest and even suggested he stay nearby so Rusty could offer him protection from other savage creatures.

Time went by, and Rusty and Lively became good friends. Since Lively had lived with people and was well educated, he taught Rusty judgment. He weaned Rusty from forest habits and gave him village manners. They were together all the time and kept others at a distance. Even the two jackals, Cautious and Crafty, could not get close to them. They could not share in the bounty of the lion's hunts and all of Rusty's animal followers were going hungry.

Now we all know that servants may leave when they see no reward and stay if there is pay. All creatures live off each other. Kings live off countries; doctors live off patients; merchants off customers; the learned off fools; thieves off the careless; and workers off everyone. Creatures set traps, wait night and day and, when given a chance, pounce like big fish on small fish.

Cautious and Crafty, robbed of their master's favour, and hungry, tried to figure out what they should do. Cautious thought: *Even when masters won't take advice, good counsellors should warn the King.* 'Besides,' he told Crafty, 'you are the one who introduced Lively to Rusty.'

'You are right,' agreed Crafty. 'Think of what happened when Cheat played tricks, or the jackal at the ram fight, or even the meddling friend.'

'How so?' asked Cautious, and Crafty told these three stories one after another. ✑

Pious and Cheat

A holy man named Pious lived in a secluded monastery. He performed sacrifices for people, who in turn gave him beautifully woven fabrics. He sold them and made a large sum of money.

Once rich, he came to trust no man. He always kept his treasure beside him for he knew that money is hard to get and keeping it is harder still.

Now a conman named Cheat noticed Pious's treasure always under his arm. 'How can I get it?' Cheat asked himself. He decided to win Pious's confidence by becoming his disciple. He vowed to be clever in his flattery.

'O holy Sir,' he said bowing low to Pious. 'All life is vanity. Can you help teach me how to escape it?'

Pious was impressed by this question and replied, 'My son, you are blessed to realize this when so young. Deep prayer is the way.'

Cheat fell to Pious's feet and asked Pious to impose a vow of poverty on him. Pious did so but told Cheat to never enter Pious's cell at night. He knew that *much is lost through careless action.* So Pious told Cheat to sleep in a thatched hut at the monastery gate.

Cheat became Pious's disciple, but Pious still kept his treasure under his arm. Cheat thought: 'Maybe I will have to kill him to get the treasure.' But then, as chance would have it, the son of an old friend of Pious came and invited him to his house for a baptism. On the way to the friend's house they had to cross a river, so Pious carefully wrapped his treasure in an old robe, prayed and gave it to Cheat for safekeeping.

The minute he had the parcel in his hands, Cheat took off with it.

Jackal at the Ram Fight

Continuing on his journey, Pious decided to take a break. He was resting peacefully when he saw a herd of rams, two of whom were fighting. They had locked horns and blood flowed from their injuries. A jackal stood between the rams, lapping up the blood.

'Well, well!' thought Pious. 'What a stupid jackal! If that jackal stays where he is and happens to come between the rams when the fight begins again, he will certainly be killed.'

The greedy jackal did not move away, was caught between the crashing heads and was killed. Feeling sorry for the jackal, Pious returned to the river to get his treasure.

However, he failed to find Cheat or his treasure, although his old robe lay where he had given it to Cheat. Pious fainted from shock.

When he came to, he started shouting, 'Cheat, Cheat! Where have you gone after robbing me?' and he started to track him down.

Weaver's Wife

As he was looking for Cheat, Pious met a Weaver who along with his wife was on his way to a nearby city to buy liquor. Pious begged the Weaver for some food and shelter. He reminded the Weaver that charity to the poor wins favour in God's eyes. Hearing the request, the Weaver told his wife, 'Go with our guest. Treat him well and respectfully. Give him food and shelter. I will go on alone to the city and return with meat and wine,' and took off.

The wife turned back home with Pious and was happy to do so for she was already thinking of another man. She gave Pious a broken down cot and said, 'Holy Sir, my girlfriend has come from the village and I must speak to her. I will be back shortly.' She put on her best clothes and left to meet her lover.

Just then she ran smack into her husband who had returned reeling drunk. She ran hurriedly back to the house and got quickly into her ordinary clothes. But the Weaver had seen her and noticed her finery. Previously he had heard gossip about her so now his anger flared and he shouted, 'You cheat! Where were you going?'

'I have been here since I left you,' she replied. 'You are a drunkard and make things up.' But the Weaver got even madder at her lies, beat her with a rod, tied her to a post, and fell into a drunken sleep.

At this moment, finding that the Weaver was asleep, the Barber's wife, the go-between friend of the Weaver's wife, came in and said: 'Hurry up! Your lover is waiting for you.' But the Weaver's wife said, 'I cannot possibly go right now.'

'For a woman of spirit,' said the Barber's wife, 'this is no way to treat a lover. The Weaver is helpless in a drunken sleep and will not wake until the morning. I will set you free and take your place. But hurry back.'

Meanwhile, Pious who lay awake, had witnessed the whole matter. Soon, the Weaver's wife came home and found to her horror that her husband had mistakenly cut off the nose of the Barber's wife thinking it was she. She freed her friend, took her position and shouted, 'Oh, you stupid fool! I am a true wife. You cannot disfigure me. May the Gods make my nose whole and if I ever had any desire for other men, may they reduce me to ashes.'

The Weaver looked at his wife's nose and was astonished. He freed his wife and tried hard to win her back. Pious had seen the whole business and was also amazed. 'Heavens!' Pious thought to himself. 'Women are very clever even as they are very wicked, all poison within and all honey without.'

At the same time, the go-between Barber's wife with her nose cut off wondered what she could do to hide her loss. Her husband who had spent the night as required

in the King's palace came home and said, 'Bring me my razor-case. People in town need my services and I have to clean up.'

His wife had a sudden idea and gave the Barber a single razor. The Barber got angry for he needed the whole case, so he flung the single razor at his wife. Immediately she seized her opportunity and ran from the house screaming, 'I am a faithful wife. But look! My husband cut off my nose. Help! Help!'

The police arrived, flogged the Barber, tied him up and took him to court with his noseless wife. The jury men asked the Barber why he had done such a terrible thing, but he was so bewildered at his plight that he said nothing. The jurymen took his silence as a sign of guilt. They believed that a guilty person would be afraid, but an innocent one would be indignant. They pronounced: 'The legal penalty for assaulting a woman is death.'

However, Pious intervened. He went to the officers of justice and said, 'You are making a big mistake. Please listen to me.' And he told all three stories. The Barber was freed, his wife punished by having her ears cut off as well, and Pious returned to the monastery muttering to himself, 'The jackal at the ram fight; I, tricked of my treasure; and the nosy friend – we all three cooked our own goose!'

Having heard Crafty's stories, Cautious asked, 'What are we to do?'

Crafty was ready with an answer. 'Our master has fallen into serious vice.'

'What are you talking about?' inquired Cautious. Crafty proceeded to count the seven truly grave vices, or as some say, types of evil:

Drinking,

Womanizing,

Hunting,

Gambling,

Verbal Abuse,

Greed

and Cruelty. The first four arise from unbridled passion, the last three from unbridled anger.

'Together,' Crafty explained, '*they form a single vice, that of Addiction.* But, really, there are five vicious situations: *Deficiency, Corruption, Addiction, Disaster and Bad Policy. Deficiency is the lack of king, minister, subjects, fortress, treasury, authority to punish, and allies. Corruption is when subjects, individually or collectively, start breaking laws.*

Addiction is divided into the love-group (drink, women, hunting, gambling) and the anger-group (unwarranted blaming of innocents, unjust taking of another's property, and unreasonable, ruthless punishment). Disaster includes an act of God, fire, flood, famine, disease, plague, mass panic and hurricanes. Bad Policy is the mistaken use of the six strategies: Peace, Alliance, Implacability, Invasion, War and Duplicity.'

'Our master Rusty has fallen into the very first vice, that of Deficiency,' said Crafty. 'He is so taken by Lively that he pays not the smallest attention to counsellors or any of the other six supports of his throne. He must be detached from Lively. No lamp, no light.'

'And how will you do that?' objected Cautious. 'You have no power!'

'My dear fellow, I am thinking of how the crow-hen killed the black snake,' replied Crafty, and told this story.

Crow-Hen and the Black Snake

Once, a Crow and his wife built their nest in a huge banyan tree. Every time the Crow-Hen had chicks, a great black snake would crawl up the hollow trunk of the tree and eat the chicks. But the poor crows would not leave. You know what they say: The deer, the coward and the crow cannot be induced to go when things go wrong, but the lion, hero and elephant always do.

Eventually, the Crow-Hen begged her husband, 'I cannot stand it any longer. There is no love like the love of children and we will never have any in this deadly place. Let us make our nest in some other tree.'

The Crow was very sad but answered, 'We have lived in this tree for a long time and cannot desert it. I will try to figure out some way to kill our enemy.'

'But this is a very poisonous snake – how can you kill him?' asked the wife.

'I know I do not have the power to do it,' replied the Crow. 'Still, I have learned friends and I will ask their advice.' So he flew to another tree under which lived a

jackal, who was a friend, and told his painful tale. 'Please, can you help me?' he asked the Jackal. 'The death of our children is unbearable for my wife and me.'

'Do not worry,' said the Jackal, 'the heartless cruelty of the vicious black snake will itself bring his end. Remember what happened to the greedy heron.'

'How so?' asked the Crow, and the Jackal told him this story.

Heron Who Liked Crabmeat

There was once a Heron who lived near a pond. He was getting very old and tried to find an easy way to catch fish. He began to loiter at the very edge of the pond, pretending to be muddled and not eating even the fish well within reach.

In the same pond lived a Crab. One day the Crab asked, 'Why aren't you catching and eating the fish?'

The Heron answered, 'Soon a great disaster will befall the pond, so I am depressed.'

'What kind of calamity?' asked the Crab.

'Today I eavesdropped on fishermen who are planning to come tomorrow or the day after with their fishing nets to catch fish here,' said the Heron. When the pond creatures heard this, they all feared for their lives and begged the Heron to save them.

'I am a bird and cannot fight men,' the Heron declared, 'but I can transfer some of you from this pond to another, a bottomless one where you would be safe.'

The pond creatures were led astray by the speech and each shouted, 'Me first! Take me first.'

Then the old crook did what the fish begged. He picked some up in his bill, carried them quite a distance to a big flat rock and ate them there. Day after day, he made the trip and had a feast while keeping the trust of the pond creatures.

One day, the Crab, who was afraid of being left behind to die, begged the Heron to take him too. The Heron, bored with eating fish, readily agreed to take him next. He picked up the Crab and flew away. When he was going to land on the usual rock ledge, the Crab asked, 'Sir, where is the pond without any bottom?'

The Heron laughed. 'See that rock? That is where all the fish found peace and now it is your turn.'

'Oh dear,' thought the Crab, '*friends or enemies, everyone serves their own ends. One should shun false and foolish friends.* The Heron is clever, but he picked me up. Now it is my turn to grab his neck with all my claws before he lands and drops me.' When the Crab did so, the Heron tried to escape, but the Crab had cut his head off.

The Crab painfully made his way back to the pond, dragging the Heron's neck.

'Why did you come back?' asked the remaining pond creatures and he told them how the Heron had fooled and betrayed them all. 'I have brought back the Heron's

neck to show you he is dead. Forget your worries. All creatures can now live in the pond quite safely.'

*

'But how will the vicious snake meet his end?' asked the Crow.

The Jackal advised: 'Go to the King's favourite spot. Seize a gold chain or necklace from any rich man who is careless. Then put it somewhere so that when it is found by the guards, the snake will be seen and killed.'

So the Crow and Crow-Hen flew away. The Crow-Hen was first to reach a pond where the King's ladies were bathing, having left their jewellery on the bank. Quickly she seized a gold chain and flew back to her tree. The King's servants had seen the theft. They picked up clubs, and ran in pursuit.

Meanwhile, the Crow-Hen quickly dropped the golden chain in the snake's hole and watched from a distance. When the King's men found the hole and the gold chain in it, they saw the black snake. They killed the snake and recovered the chain. Thereafter, the Crow and his wife lived in peace and happily raised a large family in their lifelong home.

So the saying goes, said Crafty: '*Where brute force cannot work, a shrewd device may. Some heedless men may allow a petty foe to grow unhindered, but for the intelligent, there is nothing they cannot control. Intelligence is power.* Where power joins with folly, the rabbit lives and the lion dies.'

'How so?' asked Cautious, and Crafty told this story. 🙰

Arrogant and Rabbit

There was a lion named Arrogant who was so full of himself that he killed every animal he saw just because he could. All the other forest animals – deer, boars, buffaloes, wild oxen and rabbits – got together and in despair asked Arrogant for mercy:

'Please, O King, stop your meaningless slaughter. The Holy Book says that sins in this life will have to be paid for in the life hereafter. Only fools pave the way to Hell. Please stop killing everyone and if you will but stay home, we ourselves will bring you an animal each day for food.'

The animals went on to remind Arrogant: *The King who does not overtax his subjects rules longest.* The King who tends his subjects is the only king who can become rich.

Arrogant was convinced and agreed that he would stop the killing only if an animal came to him every day. So each day at noon, an animal appeared as his dinner. Each species took its turn and provided a willing animal, old, grief-stricken, or fearful of the loss of son or wife, and ready to make a sacrifice.

On rabbit-day, the animals gave directions to a rabbit to go to the lion's den. Rabbit thought to himself: 'I wish I could kill this lion, but how can I? I am just a rabbit.' Then he thought that with wisdom, resolution and flattery, surely all enterprise would succeed.

'I can kill even a lion!' he thought.

So Rabbit started walking very slowly, knowing he would be late, all the way trying to figure out a way to kill the lion. Very late in the day he appeared before the lion who was very hungry and very angry. The lion was thinking: 'I must start killing animals first thing in the morning!'

Rabbit approached quietly and bowed. The Lion saw that the Rabbit was not only late but was also really too small for a meal and he shouted,: 'You rascal. First, you are too tiny for a meal. Second, you are late. Because of this wickedness, I am going to kill you and tomorrow I will go back to killing every animal I see, whether I am hungry or not.'

The Rabbit bowed lower and said, 'Master, the fault is not mine nor of the other animals. Please listen to the cause!'

'OK, hurry up,' said Arrogant. 'What do you have to say?'

'All the animals knew today was rabbit-day,' the Rabbit said, 'and because I am quite small, they sent me

with five other rabbits. But mid-journey there sprang from a great hole in the ground another lion who asked: "Where are you going?" I explained that we were being sent as the dinner for Lion Arrogant, according to our agreement. "Is that so?" the other lion said. "This forest belongs to me! All forest animals, without exception, must bow to me. Arrogant is a thief. Bring him here at once and whichever of us proves stronger will be king of all animals in this forest."'

'I,' said Rabbit, 'am here at his order.'

'So take me to this lion,' said Arrogant. 'Where there is no prospect of a great and sure reward and the risk is great and sure instead, he should not have picked a fight!'

'But, Master, he came out of a fortress and *an enemy in a fortress is hard to beat*,' remarked Rabbit, to which Arrogant replied, 'Show me the imposter even if he is hiding in a fortress. I will kill him. For *the strongest man who fails to crush disease or foe, will later be destroyed by that which he permits to grow.*'

'Follow me, Master,' and the Rabbit took Arrogant to a well where he said to the lion, 'Master, who can stand up to Your Majesty? The moment he saw you, the thief crawled into his hole. Come, I will show him to you.' Rabbit showed him the well where Arrogant, big fool he, seeing his own reflection and hearing the echo of his own roar much magnified, hurled himself into the well, falling to his death.

Rabbit, in high spirits, returned to the other animals, gave them the good news, accepted their compliments, and lived to be a very old rabbit.

*

'But that is a special case. Even if Rabbit was successful, *the weak should not deal fraudulently with the strong*,' objected Cautious.

'*Weak or strong, one must make up one's mind to act with vigour,*' retorted Crafty. '*Unceasing effort, not fate, brings success.* In fact, the very Gods befriend those who always strive and not even Brahma sees through well-devised deceit. Remember the weaver who was persistent and won the Princess.'

'How was that?' asked Cautious, and Crafty told this story.

Weaver Who Loved a Princess

The Weaver and the Chariot-Maker were good friends. They lived and worked in Sugarcane City. They were master craftsmen who earned enough to not be bothered about keeping an account of their money. They wore fashionable clothes, were always well-groomed and moved freely in high society.

One day, there was a big city festival and everyone put on their best and went to the fair. So did the Weaver and the Chariot-Maker. As they wandered around, looking at people and things, they got a glimpse of Princess Lovely. She was seated, surrounded by girlfriends, at the window of the King's handsome stone palace. She was drop-dead gorgeous, with extraordinary grace and an unusually pretty face. The Weaver was struck by Cupid and could not see anything but the princess and her beauty. When he got back home, he lay in bed, reciting poems that might be able to express his love.

When the Chariot-Maker arrived the next morning, he saw the unkempt, love-sick Weaver and quickly diagnosed the problem. 'The King belongs to the warrior class, while you are a tradesman,' he warned. 'Have you no respect for the holy law?'

'But,' the Weaver replied, 'the holy law also allows a warrior three wives. Perhaps one wife of the King may be a woman of my class, which would justify my love for her daughter, the Princess Lovely.' Seeing his friend in such an awful state, the Chariot-Maker relented and told the Weaver that he would try and figure out a way by which the Weaver could win his lady.

The following morning, true to his word, the Chariot-Maker brought with him a brand-new mechanical bird, which looked like Garuda, the golden eagle of God Vishnu. It was made of wood, brightly painted, with all kinds of neat plugs and levers.

'My bird,' he told the Weaver, 'will take you where you want to go: push in that plug to start it and pull it out to stop. Tonight, when the world sleeps, dress up like Vishnu, mount this Garuda-like bird and fly to the palace to meet your Princess who sleeps alone on the palace balcony.'

So, just past midnight, the Weaver followed his friend's instructions. The Princess was thrilled to be chosen as the loved one of God Vishnu. She did not know, of course, that it was a weaver dressed as Vishnu. He told her that she was really his wife earthbound by a curse and that he had come to wed her in a marriage ceremony common in heaven. So she married him that night. Every night the Weaver would come to meet her and leave in the morning.

Eventually, the guards in the women's quarters realized this and, fearing for their lives, reported it to the King. 'O King,' they said, 'we beg for your protection for we need to tell you a secret.'

The King agreed and the guards told him that Princess Lovely was meeting a man every night. 'What do you want us to do?' they asked.

The King was troubled and contemplated how from the time a daughter is born to him, a father worries about picking the right husband for her. It sure is difficult to be the father of a girl! Whenever a poem, or daughter, is born, the creator is filled with doubt: *'Will she reach the right hands? Will she please as she stands? And what will the critics say?'*

The King went to the Queen for advice. She went straight to their daughter and started to scold her. 'You are a wicked girl! You have brought disgrace to this royal family. Tell me the truth!'

And the Princess told her the story of the Weaver disguised as Vishnu. The Queen was delighted, believing that God Vishnu had married her daughter. She hurried to tell the King and they happily decided to hide that night and witness Vishnu's coming.

When they realized that their daughter had truthfully described Vishnu's visits, the King said to the Queen, 'You and I are truly blessed to have God Vishnu in love

with our daughter. Now, through the power of our son-in-law, I shall be able to rule the whole world.'

At this time, representatives came to collect the annual tribute for Emperor Valour, who was Lord of the whole south, all nine million nine hundred thousand villages. But the King, full of his newfound relationship with Vishnu, did not treat them with the customary humility and respect.

The representatives got angry: 'Pay up, King. Have you become a superman with special powers that you can afford to irritate Emperor Valour, himself a Death-God?' The King ignored them and they returned to their country exaggerating their insult a thousandfold and making their master very angry indeed.

Emperor Valour got his troops together and marched northward to wage war against the King of Sugarcane City. He arrived uninterrupted and destroyed everything in sight. But the King was not concerned. His people saw that they were surrounded by Emperor Valour's troops and begged their King to do something. 'Why are you so unconcerned?' they asked and the King replied, 'Wait until the morning.'

Meanwhile, he sent for Princess Lovely and affectionately approached her. 'Dear daughter,' he said, 'we are relying on your husband's power to end the attack by our enemy. Please ask the Great Vishnu to vanquish our foe.' When Weaver-Vishnu came that night, Lovely passed on the King's request.

The Weaver laughed and said, 'Tell the King not to worry. In the morning, Vishnu will kill your enemies with his powerful weapon, the magical discus.'

The King was overjoyed when he heard what Vishnu had said and made a proclamation to his people: 'Whatever you grab from the battlefield tomorrow will remain your personal property.' The people were delighted and sang the King's praises.

Meanwhile, the Weaver was debating with himself: 'If I fly off on my machine, I will never see my love again and her parents will be killed by Emperor Valour. If I do battle, I will meet death and with it my love will die. Either way, I will die – of lost love or lost battle. Besides, it is possible that Emperor Valour's army will be fooled and thinking me to be Vishnu, will flee.'

When the Weaver decided upon battle, the real Garuda reported to the real God Vishnu about the imposter in Sugarcane City and said, 'If the Weaver dies in battle, there will be a scandal. Men will say that God Vishnu was slain by a man. People will lose faith and offerings will diminish. Atheists will destroy temples. What do you want to do?'

'You make a good case,' said Vishnu. 'Perhaps we had better lend the Weaver our powers to slay Emperor Valour.'

When the battle began and the Weaver-Vishnu swooped down on the mechanical bird-Garuda, everyone was amazed. The other Gods too came to witness the scene. Emperor Valour was slain and all earthly kings came to beg Weaver-Vishnu for mercy.

Weaver-Vishnu proclaimed, 'Your people are secure from now on, but only if you obey the commands of the local king.'

From then on the Weaver enjoyed all the advantages of being Princess Lovely's husband.

Having heard the whole story, Cautious understood that Crafty was determined to proceed against King Rusty and gave his blessing.

Crafty went to see King Rusty. 'Where have you been?' asked Rusty.

'O King, there is urgent business for you,' said Crafty. 'I have unwelcome news, which I would much rather not have brought, but *devoted servants need to speak the unpleasant truth to their masters.*'

'What are you talking about?' asked Rusty.

'Lively, whom you have trusted, has been heard to speak treason,' Crafty said. 'Now that he knows you so well, he plans to kill you and seize the royal power for himself. I am here to warn Your Majesty, who is my lord and master.'

Rusty was thunderstruck and devastated. Crafty, correctly judging his state of mind, went on: 'No king should ever delegate to one individual all the powers of the state, for eventually such a person will want to become king himself.'

'Lively is my servant,' said Rusty. 'Why should he have a change of heart towards me? Once dear is always dear.'

'For that very reason,' went on Crafty, '*there is a serious flaw in the business of getting on in the world. Everyone, of high birth or low, when given a chance will aspire to seize the throne.* Your good feelings for Lively are misplaced. *Never leave tried and loyal servants and counsellors for someone new and unknown,* as Lively was to you.'

'But,' interrupted Rusty, 'broken promises are a shame and I promised Lively protection.'

Crafty replied, 'Remember, my Lord, *caress a rascal as you will, he was and is a rascal still; you cannot straighten a mongrel's tail. You must always listen to sound advice no matter who gives it.* Remember the story of the ungrateful man.'

'Which one is that?' asked Rusty, and Crafty told the following story.

Grateful Animals and Ungrateful Man

There once was a poor Brahmin named Sacrifice. Every day his wife would nag: 'Mr Layabout, your children are starving and you do nothing but hang around. Go somewhere, no matter where, get some food and hurry back.'

Weary of listening to his wife's nagging, Sacrifice went off on a long journey that took him through a deep forest. While wandering in it, hungry and thirsty, he came upon an old well, pretty much hidden by grass growing around it. When he looked down into the well, he saw a tiger, a monkey, a snake and a man at the very bottom. Of course, they also saw him.

The Tiger shouted: 'Noble Sir, there is great merit in saving someone's life. Will you please pull me out so that I may live with my wife, sons, relatives and friends.'

'But I am scared of you.'

To which the Tiger replied, '*Forgiveness is granted even*

to the killer and the lying sinner, but there is none ever given to the ingrate. I promise by a triple oath that you will never be in any danger from me. Have pity and pull me out.'

The Brahmin thought that even if disaster results from saving a life, it leads to salvation, and he pulled the Tiger out.

Next, the Monkey asked, 'Holy Sir, pull me out too,' and the Brahmin pulled him out as well.

Then the Snake asked, 'What about me?.'

The Brahmin answered, 'I tremble at the mere sound of your hiss, how much more at your touch!'

'But', said the Snake, 'we are not free agents. We bite only under orders. I bind myself by a triple oath that you need have no fear of me.' The Brahmin pulled him out too.

Then the animals told the Brahmin: 'That man down there is a bad, bad, man. Do not trust him. Do not pull him out.'

The Tiger then invited the Brahmin to his home on the north slope of a nearby mountain so he could return the Brahmin's kindness. And the Monkey invited him to his home beside the waterfall. And the Snake reminded the Brahmin to remember him in any emergency. All three went away.

Meanwhile, the man kept shouting from the bottom of the well, 'Brahmin, pull me out too!'

In the end, the Brahmin took pity on him, and thinking he was a man like he was, pulled him out too.

The man said, 'I am a goldsmith and live nearby. If you have any gold to be worked into shape, bring it to me and I will get you a good price.' Then he left.

Sacrifice continued his journey but found nothing whatever to take back to his wife. Dejected, he started for home, but then remembered the Monkey. So he paid him a visit, found the Monkey at home and received delicious fruits that revived him. Besides this, the Monkey assured him that if he ever needed fruit again, he should come to him without hesitation.

The Brahmin then went to visit the Tiger, who surprised him with a gift of a gold necklace he had taken off a prince whom he had killed the day before. The Brahmin took it readily, thinking he would go to the Goldsmith who would do him the favour of selling it for him. He started for the Goldsmith's house.

The Goldsmith asked the Brahmin, 'How may I help you?' and the Brahmin gave him the necklace, which the Goldsmith recognized as the one he had made for the prince the year before. Asking the Brahmin to wait at his house, he took it to the King. On seeing it, the King concluded that the Brahmin had killed his son, and ordered the Brahmin be captured and hanged the next day.

When the Brahmin was caught, he realized that he had not done what the Tiger, the Monkey and the Snake had advised and so that dreadful, ungrateful man had brought him down. He also remembered the Snake who, as promised, appeared at once and asked, 'How can I serve you?'

'Free me from these fetters,' begged the Brahmin.

'I will bite the King's dear Queen and arrange things so that she will recover only by your touch,' said the Snake. 'Then you will be set free.' This, the Snake did.

So that is what happened. While freeing the Brahmin, the King asked him, 'How did you get the gold necklace?' The Brahmin told him the whole story. When the King understood the facts, he arrested the Goldsmith, gave the Brahmin a thousand villages and made him a privy counsellor. Sacrifice gathered his family, relatives and friends around him. A wise man, he took delight in everyday living and went on to acquire great merit and authority by performing many services to others.

Having told the story, Crafty continued, 'My Lord and King, you associate with Lively, making a very serious mistake that results in the neglect of *the three things worth living for: virtue, money and love.* Despite my protests, my Lord and King goes his wilful way, ignoring my advice. In the future, when the crash comes, do not blame me.'

'So should I not warn him?' asked the Lion.

'Oh, no,' replied Crafty. '*It is only wise to warn an enemy by action, not word.*'

'After all,' said Rusty, 'he is a grass nibbler. I am a carnivore. How can Lively hurt me?'

'That's just the point,' said Crafty. 'Even the weak but malicious fool can hurt you in unexpected ways. Lively, living beside you, spreads his dung far and wide. In it worms will breed. The worms will find cracks in your battle-scars and will bore deep. As the proverb goes "*With no stranger share your house*: Leap, the flea, killed Creep, the louse."'

'How so?' asked Rusty, and Crafty told him this story.

Leap and Creep

In the palace of a famous King, there was a magnificent bed with all kinds of comforts. In a corner of the quilted bedspread there lived a female louse called Creep. Every night, surrounded by a very large family of children and grandchildren, she drank the King's blood as he slept. On such a healthy diet she had grown plump and very attractive.

One day a flea named Leap drifted in on the breeze through the open window of the King's bedroom and landed on the bed. Leap was delighted with the luxurious bed and hopped around happily, testing its qualities, until he suddenly met Creep.

'Where did you come from?' shouted Creep. 'This is the King's bed. Be gone at once.'

'Lady,' responded Leap, 'you should remember that I am a guest, even if unexpected, and the whole world treats guests with due hospitality and respect. I have figured out that this is a rich and healthy man's bed. Therefore, with your permission, I will sample his rich and healthy blood combining pleasure and gain.'

'No', said Creep, 'you don't know your position and like a fool forgetting his duty, time and place, you will fall by the wayside.'

But Leap fell to his knees and again beseeched Creep's favour. She, remembering that *spurning a suppliant enemy was always a mistake*, finally gave in. But she did caution Leap, 'Do not feed at the wrong time and the wrong place.'

'What is the wrong time and the wrong place,' asked Leap. 'I have no idea.'

'When the King's body is overcome by drink, tiredness, or deep sleep, then one may quietly bite him on the feet. That is the right time and the right place.'

However, Leap did not bother to follow the advice. He was hungry and the King had just gotten into bed when he bit him in the lower back. As if stung by a hornet, the King jumped up and shouted to his servants, 'Something bit me! Hunt through this bed until you find the culprit and kill it.'

Leap quickly hid in a crevice in the bed, so when the servants searched the bedding they found only Creep and her family whom they killed right away.

'And that is why I say,' said Crafty 'never share your home with a stranger.' In addition, my Lord and King, you do wrong in neglecting the servants who are yours by inheritance. Remember whoever leaves his friends to cultivate strangers will ultimately perish like Fierce-Howl.'

'How so?' asked Rusty, and Crafty told this story. ✍

Blue Jackal

A jackal named Fierce-Howl lived in a cave just outside a fairly big city. One day he went hunting for food. He was starving, his throat hurt, and he wandered into the city after dark. Right away, the city dogs surrounded him, snapped at his heels with their sharp-pointed teeth and terrified him with their menacing bark. Trying to escape, he ran this way and that, until he reached the home of a dyer. He rushed to hide in the dyer's work area and accidentally fell into an indigo vat. Seeing him fall in, the dogs went home.

However, Fierce-Howl's time was not yet up. Eventually, the jackal managed to climb out of the vat of indigo dye and escaped into a forest.

There, all the nearby forest animals who caught a glimpse of him, dyed as he was a bright indigo blue, cried out in awe: 'What animal is this with such an extraordinary colour?' Their eyes reflected their terror and they shouted out this news through the whole forest: 'We are going to disappear. For the proverb says: *When you do not know the origins, character or strength of a possible enemy, it is best not to rely on luck.'*

Now, Fierce-Howl understood their dismay and called out, 'Why do you flee in terror? God Indra, knowing that you have no ruler right now, has chosen me to be your King. Rest assured and come live safely with me.'

Hearing this, the lions, tigers, leopards, monkeys, rabbits, gazelles, jackals and all other forest animals humbly bowed to Fierce-Howl and said, 'Master, tell us our duties.'

Thereupon, the jackal appointed the lion prime minister and the tiger lord of the bedchamber, while he made the leopard the custodian of the King's snuffbox, the elephant the doorkeeper, and the monkey the bearer of the royal parasol. But to all the jackals, his own kind, he ordered a flogging and immediate exile.

Then Fierce-Howl went about enjoying a king's glory, while the lions and others killed animals for food and laid them before him. These he divided and distributed to all, after the manner of kings.

Time passed pleasantly. One day, Fierce-Howl was sitting in court when he heard the beloved loud sound made by a pack of jackals who were howling nearby in unison. Hearing it, his skin tingled, his eyes filled with tears of joy, and in kinship he leapt to his feet and began to howl in a piercing tone. When the lions and all other animals heard him, they realized that he was only a jackal. They stood around for a minute, shamefaced and downcast, then said to themselves, 'Look, we have been deceived by this jackal. Let the fellow be killed.'

When Fierce-Howl heard this verdict, he tried to flee but was torn to bits by a tiger.

Then Rusty asked Crafty, 'How will I know that Lively is treacherous and wishes me harm? What is his fighting technique?'

Crafty answered readily. 'Normally, he comes into your presence quite relaxed. If, today, he approaches timidly, but obviously ready to pierce with his horns, then the King will know that he has treachery on his mind.' Crafty then left to go and visit Bull.

Crafty presented himself sluggish and dejected to Lively.

Lively noticed his mood and asked, 'My friend, are you in good spirits?'

To which Crafty replied 'How can a dependent be in good spirits? *A never-ending train of sorrows follows those in service of a king. There are five types of people who experience death-in-life: the poor man, the sick man, the exile, the fool and the servant of a king. This person lives a dog's life, but dogs can do things they like, whereas a slave must obey his king.'*

Listening to this, Lively figured out that Crafty had a hidden purpose in mind, so he asked: 'Tell me what is bothering you.'

Crafty replied, 'Well, you are my friend, so I cannot help telling you what is in your best interest. Rusty is mad at you. He said today, "I will kill Lively and invite all who eat meat to a feast." Of course, on hearing such words I fell into deep despair. Now you must do what this crisis warrants.'

Lively was thunderstruck and fell into a deep sadness. As he grew more and more troubled, he became panic-stricken and said, 'If one has given cause for enmity, one may recover by removing it, but how can one placate the anger of a mind that is filled with hate without any cause? What wrong have I ever done our Master Rusty?'

'Friend,' said Crafty, 'kings injure without cause and are always looking for the most vulnerable spot of any possible opponent.'

'True, very true,' said Lively. 'I should have known *no blessing comes without some pain*. The fault is mine. *I chose a false friend. Harsh talk, untimely action and false friends should not be ignored*. Think of the swan who was sleeping among the lilies and was killed by the arrow.'

'How was that?' asked Crafty, and Lively told him this story.

Swan and Owl

A Swan lived along the edge of a big lake. He led a good life with many pastimes. One day an owl visited him. Surprised, the Swan asked the Owl, 'Where are you from and why are you here?'

The Owl replied, 'I have heard about your many famous virtues.' The Swan was flattered and readily invited the Owl to stay with him for as long as he wished. So the Swan and the Owl from then on lived pleasantly together for many years.

However, one day, the Owl announced that he was going back home and added that if the Swan ever wanted to visit him, he would be most welcome.

Many years passed, the Swan grew old, and eventually decided that a change would be good for him. So he went to visit the Owl. He found the Owl not only much older but living in an ugly hole and quite blind in the daytime. 'My dear Owl, remember me?' asked the Swan. 'I am your old friend, the Swan. I've come for a visit.'

The Owl answered, 'I don't go out in the day, but we can meet at sunset.' The Swan had to wait a long time and after a brief chat, he fell asleep among the lilies quite close to the Owl's nest hole.

As it happened, a contractor and his crew were spending the night nearby. The contractor rose early and blew the whistle to leave from the campsite. The Owl immediately responded with a loud piercing hoot and then dived back into his hole. The contractor, taking the hoot as an evil omen, ordered a crew member, an archer who could take aim by sound, to shoot his sharp arrow in the Owl's direction. The arrow, alas, pierced the sleeping Swan and he died.

After telling the story, Lively went on: 'King Rusty was all honey in the beginning, but now he is full of poison. I sure have learned a lesson about *false friends who deceive with warm praise in front of you and harsh criticism behind your back.* I am a vegetarian bull, how can I have a true friend who eats meat? Wise men rightly say: *When two are of equal wealth and status, marriage and friendship thrives, but not between rich and poor.* I have entered a false friend's lair and will forfeit my life. I should have remembered how Ugly's trust was abused.'

'How was that?' asked Crafty, and Lively told him this story.

Gullible Camel

There was once a merchant who loaded valuable fabrics on the back of a hundred camels and set out to trade. As they were crossing a forest, one of his camels, named Ugly, hurt his ankle and had to be left behind. Poor Ugly limped around in pain, ate what grass he could find, and before long got some of his strength back and went deeper into the forest.

In that jungle there lived a lion named Haughty, who had three dependents: a leopard, a jackal and a crow. They followed him around and survived on his leftovers. Haughty had never seen a camel and asked the Crow to find out what had brought the exotic creature to his forest. When the Crow did so, Haughty felt sorry for Ugly and promised him safe conduct.

One day Haughty was himself badly injured in a fight with an elephant whose tusk had pierced his side, which meant he could not kill animals for food for himself and his followers. So he told the others: 'You will have to fend for yourselves. But if you kill a big animal, I will help you cut it up so all of us can share it.'

So the four animals went in search for a suitable animal for food. When they did not find any, they thought of killing Ugly.

'But,' said the Crow, 'the Master promised the Camel his personal safety.'

'So he did,' answered the Jackal. 'I will go talk to him.' When he found Haughty, he said, 'We are starving and too tired to go on searching for an animal to eat. You too need food. What do you say to eating Ugly's flesh?'

'How dare you!' said Haughty. 'I promised him safe conduct, the most valuable of life's gifts.'

'Yes, Master, I understand your situation,' said the Jackal. 'But no one will blame you if Ugly volunteers to die for your well-being. Otherwise, you will have to eat one of us, your faithful servants who have been with you for a long time.'

'Very well,' said Haughty, 'you may do what you want.'

The Jackal returned to the others and convinced them that as loyal servants their only option was to offer themselves as food to their Master. First, the Crow offered himself: 'Pray eat me and prolong your life at least for a day.'

The Jackal quickly objected, 'But you are too small,' and went on to offer himself: 'Please, Master, use my body to lengthen your life and thus make my sacrifice my ticket to heaven.'

At which the Leopard interrupted: 'You too are not big enough to feed us. Master, make way for me and my loyalty, and grant me glory on earth as well as an everlasting home in heaven.'

Hearing this, poor simple Ugly thought to himself, 'Well, they may have used fancy words to volunteer to die, but the Master did not kill a single one of them. So I will do the same and, no doubt, all three will contradict me.'

So he said to the Leopard, 'Now it is my turn,' and turned to Haughty. 'Master, you surely should not eat them. Pray prolong your life with mine and give me the honour and rewards of the sacrifice.' At which point, the Lion gave the order for Ugly to be killed, and everyone feasted on poor gullible Ugly.

After telling Crafty the story, Lively went on brooding. 'But *a king with false advisors is no good for his dependents in the long run. It is better to have a vulture as a king advised by swans, than a swan as king advised by vultures who always offer evil advice that ruins the king in the end.* Remember the lion and the carpenter.'

'Why?' asked Crafty and Lively told another story. 🖎

Lion and Carpenter

There lived a Carpenter who liked to break for lunch and go every day to a nearby forest with his wife to eat, and fell some trees for wood. They enjoyed their time together. One day, a lion named Spotless came upon the Carpenter and his wife. The quick-thinking Carpenter, seeing the lion, decided it was probably wiser to face the lion than flee. So he bowed low to the lion and said, 'Welcome, friend. Please join us for lunch. My wife has cooked a delicious meal.'

The lion considered the respectful invitation and graciously replied: 'Although I am a meat-eater, I will be polite and have a taste. What kind of dainty snacks do you have to offer?'

The Carpenter gave him all the choice pieces of his own lunch. Spotless enjoyed the novelties and promised the Carpenter and his wife safe conduct through his forest. In return, the Carpenter invited the lion to come and have lunch with him every day. 'But, please come alone,' he requested the lion.

In this way Spotless and the Carpenter spent their lunchtime every day in good fellowship. However, the lion's followers, the Jackal and the Crow, who lived off the lion's leftovers were going hungry, so they approached the lion. 'Please, Master, where do you go every lunchtime? How come you return looking pleased?' Spotless readily told them about his new-found friend, the Carpenter, with whom he ate a delicious lunch cooked by the Carpenter's wife.

The Jackal and Crow immediately began plotting to kill the Carpenter because he would make a good meal that would last them a long time. But Spotless overheard them and scolded them: 'How can you think of such treachery? You know I promised the Carpenter protection. However, if you like, you can accompany me next time and I will get a tasty morsel for you too.'

So the three set off at lunchtime the next day to find the Carpenter. While they were still far away, the Carpenter saw them coming, and he and his wife quickly climbed up a tall tree. The lion came close and shouted, 'Why are you up in the tree? I am your friend – Spotless.'

The Carpenter stayed in the tree. 'Your Jackal is not trustworthy and the Crow has a sharp beak. I do not like your friends!'

'So,' said Lively, '*a king with false advisors can bring harm to his dependents.*'

And he continued to think aloud, 'What should I do? I suppose I must prepare to do battle.'

When Crafty heard this, he thought, 'Lively has sharp horns and is very strong. He could actually strike down the Master. Then, what would happen to me? I had better dissuade Lively from fighting.'

So he said to Lively, 'Don't be hasty. *Without first finding out an enemy's strength, you could lose.* Remember the sandpiper bested the sea.'

'How come?' asked Lively, and Crafty told this story. ✑

Sandpiper and the Sea

A sandpiper named Brag and his wife called Steady lived by the sea. The sea was full of water creatures: small fish, big fish, all kinds of shellfish including oysters, and even seals and sharks. When it was time for Steady to lay her eggs, she requested Brag to find her a safe spot.

'Why?' asked Brag. 'This little inlet has been our home for ages. Lay your eggs here.'

'No way!' she responded. 'Right there is the mighty Sea. He may send a high tide one day and wash away my newborn babies.'

But Brag continued to argue, 'The Sea knows me. Surely the mighty Sea will not show enmity towards me! How could he be so foolish?'

Steady, however, laughed, saying: 'Stop boasting. *How can you fail to judge your own strength and weakness? Although it is hard to know oneself, accurate self-assessment keeps the wise safe in times of danger. It is best to take advice from those who are your true friends.* Remember the foolish turtle who lost his hold on the stick, and died?'

'How did that happen?' asked Brag, and Steady told
this story.

Turtle and Two Ganders

A turtle named Shell-Back and his two friends, ganders called Skinny and Stocky, lived in a small lake surrounded by low hills.

One year, as they were faced with a twelve-year-long drought, the two ganders began to worry: 'This lake will go dry. We need to find another body of water. But first, let us say goodbye properly to our dear old friend, Shell-Back.'

When they called on the turtle and told him they were thinking of leaving, he objected strongly. 'I am a water-dweller. When the lake goes dry, I will perish from loss of water and friends. Please rescue me. The drought just means no ready food for you, but it means no life for me. Loss of life is far more important than loss of good, ready food.'

'How can we help you?' asked Skinny and Stocky. 'You are a water creature without wings and we travel by flying.'

Shell-Back, however, had an idea. 'Bring a stick of wood,' he requested.

When they did, he explained to them: 'I will grip the middle of the stick with my teeth. You two take hold of

each end with your beaks and fly through the sky until you see another lake with water that you like.'

'But' the ganders warned, 'you will not be able to say a word on the journey, or you will fall to your death!'

'Not to worry', said the turtle, 'I promise to be silent.'

So the three friends started on their journey. As they flew over a nearby city, the people below shouted to one another: 'What on earth are the geese carrying?'

On hearing the shouts below, the turtle asked his friends, 'What are the people shouting about?' The minute he opened his mouth, the foolish turtle fell to his death.

*

Having told the story of Shell-Back, Steady added, *'Forethought and ready wit always win and the person who accepts his fate always loses.'*

'How so?' asked Brag and Steady told the story of the three fish.

Forethought, Ready Wit and Fatalist

There were three full-grown fish named Forethought, Ready Wit and Fatalist, who were close friends and lived in a big pond. One day, Forethought was swimming close to the bank where some fishermen were standing and talking. Since they were obvious enemies, Forethought decided to eavesdrop.

'Lots of fish in this pond, so tomorrow we will fish here,' one of the fishermen said to another.

'Oh dear,' said Forethought to himself, 'these fishermen will soon be here. I will have to take Ready Wit and Fatalist away from here to another lake.' So he went to his friends and told them what he heard.

Immediately Ready Wit said, 'I have lived here a long time and like this lake. I do not want to move. So I had better figure out a way to protect myself from the fishermen.'

And Fatalist simply said, 'Perhaps the fishermen won't come here. There are other lakes they can fish in. Besides,

one should not keep making plans, for quite often they turn out to be unnecessary. I am going to do nothing.'

When Forethought understood that his friends had made up their minds, he swam upstream from the lake to another pond all by himself.

The next day, the fishermen showed up with large nets and caught many fish including Ready Wit and Fatalist. Ready Wit, while still in the water, played dead, and so when the fishermen checked the nets they quickly threw the dead-seeming fish back into the water for they only wanted fresh fish.

Of course, they killed and prepared Fatalist for their dinner.

*

However, the sandpiper, Brag, was still adamant. 'Why do you think I'm like Fatalist? I can and will protect you. Don't worry.' So Steady gave in and laid her eggs by the small inlet. In time they hatched safely. But the mighty Sea had been listening all this time to the sandpiper couple.

'This Brag really is very conceited,' the Sea thought, 'let me put his strength to the test.'

One day when Brag and Steady left to go hunt for their food, the Sea sent a higher than usual tide and took away their chicks. When they returned and Steady found the nest empty, she was distraught.

'See, I told you so!' she told Brag. 'The Sea has taken my eggs. I warned you more than once. Now I am so miserable that I shall die.'

'Please', said Brag, 'wait until you see what I can do. I will dry up that villainous Sea with my bill.'

'How can you?' replied Steady. 'That's impossible!'

Still Brag insisted. He said, '*Success depends on iron-strong willpower,* nothing else.'

Finally Steady gave in, saying, 'OK, but at least call on other birds for help before you begin this enormous task. *For there is always strength in large numbers.* Even the sparrow, with help from the woodpecker, gnat and frog, brought down the elephant.'

'How did that happen?' asked Brag, and Steady told this story.

Sparrow versus Elephant

A Sparrow and his wife lived in a thick forest and had their nest pretty high up in a maple tree. That is where the Sparrow-Hen laid her eggs. One day in late spring, an elephant who was bothered by the heat took shelter under the same tree. He was blinded by sweat and, without thinking, pulled at the main branch with his long trunk, broke it and brought down the nest.

The eggs were smashed, but the Sparrows themselves made a narrow escape.

The Sparrow-Hen was devastated at the loss of her chicks and could not stop crying. A Woodpecker friend of hers came over and tried to console her with this advice: 'My dear friend, why cry in vain? As the saying goes, *the only difference between the wise and the foolish is that the wise do not cry for what is past, dead or lost.*'

'That is a good practice,' said the Sparrow-Hen, 'but it was the elephant who carelessly killed my chicks. Why don't you think of a way to kill him? It would lessen my sorrow to see him pay for what he did.'

The Woodpecker knew that *a friend in need is a friend indeed, for when you do not need anything, everyone is your friend*. So she decided she must somehow help her friend the Sparrow-Hen. 'Let me see what I can do,' said the Woodpecker. 'I will go see my friend, the Gnat, and bring her back to figure out together how to kill the elephant.'

When the Gnat understood the problem, she said, 'There is only one way to proceed. I have a very good friend, a Frog. Let us go ask his advice. Plans devised together by true friends usually work out well.'

So all three went to the Frog and told him the whole story. 'One creature, even if it is an elephant, is weak compared to the combined strength of many. You, Gnat, must go and buzz enticingly in the elephant's ears so that he will close his eyes. Then you, Woodpecker, will peck out his eyes. After that, I will trick him into thinking that there is water nearby that might give him relief. Instead, I will lead him to the edge of a deep pit I know, where he will fall in and die.'

'That is exactly how the three friends killed the elephant.' Steady told Brag.

*

Hearing this story, the Sandpiper agreed: 'All right, all right! I will assemble my friends and together we will dry up the Sea.' At which time, Brag called on each and every bird he knew and told them how the Sea had destroyed his chicks.

As they all started to beat their wings, one bird said, 'It will be hard to dry the sea by beating our wings. Why don't we fill up the sea with clods of clay and gravel instead?'

Then an old bird suggested, 'Why don't we ask the advice of the wise Old Gander who lives near the big banyan tree. *You know they say it was old-timers with long experience who gave the wise advice that freed the wild-goose flock held captive.*'

'How was that?' asked the birds, and the old bird told this story.

Clever Old Gander

There was a big fig tree that stood in the middle of the forest and had many broad branches. In this tree lived a flock of wild geese. In time, there grew a vicious creeping vine underneath it. Noticing it, the Old Gander said, 'This vine that is beginning its climb up our fig tree bodes ill. Someone could easily climb up it one day and kill us. We should cut it down while it is still thin and easily cut.' But the geese disliked his advice and decided to do nothing. The vine eventually wound around and all the way up the trunk of the fig tree.

One day, when the geese were away searching for food, a hunter came by, easily climbed up with the help of the vine, laid a trap and went home for the night. When the geese returned, they all got caught in the net.

'Oh dear,' the Old Gander thought, 'the very disaster I predicted has come true and we are all caught and in danger of dying.'

The geese, realizing their mistake, begged him to let

bygones be bygones. 'Please Sir, help us,' they begged him. 'What should we do now?'

The Old Gander replied, 'If you are really ready to take my advice, play dead when the villainous hunter returns. Thinking us dead, he will simply throw each of us to the ground and not bind us. When the last one is on the ground, and he is still up in the tree, we must all rise up together and fly away as fast as we can.'

Early the next morning the hunter arrived and saw the 'dead' flock of geese and threw them down one by one. The geese followed the advice of the clever Old Gander, waited for the last goose to hit the ground, and then flew away together.

*

When the story was over, all the birds decided to visit the Old Gander themselves. They told him how sad and upset they were about Steady's chicks being taken away.

The Old Gander replied, 'Our King is Garuda, the Bird-King. We need to arouse his feelings with a loud chorus of weeping and wailing so that he feels our sorrow and grieves with us. When he does that, he will remove our pain.' So all the birds went to find Garuda.

As it happened, Garuda was on his way to meet his master, God Vishnu, to prepare for a mighty battle between Gods and Demons. The birds petitioned Garuda for help, pointing out that they were weak and one of their own had been badly treated by his servant, the Sea.

'O Divine Garuda,' they requested, 'please help us. The chicks were stolen when the Sandpipers were out looking for food. As you know, *the poor must feed in secret, out of sight*. After all, we cannot do so in plain sight. Remember the Ram was killed by the Lion for doing so.'

'Remind me,' said Garuda, and an old bird told this story.

Lion and Ram

There was once a Ram who got separated from his flock and roamed alone in the woods. He looked very strong with his thick fleece and big horns, so most animals left him alone and he, in turn, was quite content being all by himself.

One day, a Lion with a large retinue, saw him looking very confident and powerful, and was somewhat scared because he had never before seen a ram in his woods. So much so that the Lion thought to leave the Ram alone and backed away from confrontation.

Later that same day, however, the Lion saw the same Ram quietly grazing among the trees. 'What!' he thought. 'The creature is a grass-eater and as his strength can only depend on his diet, he cannot be very powerful.' So the Lion quickly attacked and killed the Ram.

*

Just then, God Vishnu's messenger arrived and relayed an order to go at once to the divine city. Garuda replied, 'What will the Master do with such a poor servant as me?'

'Better come,' said the messenger. 'No need to show your pride, even if you don't like God Vishnu's order.'

'But,' insisted Garuda, 'the Sea, the resting place of God Vishnu himself, has stolen the Sandpipers' chicks and the birds are my servants. Tell God Vishnu that if I don't scold the Sea, I cannot be a worthy servant of God to him.'

God Vishnu, hearing about Garuda's anger at the Sea, decided to come and talk to Garuda himself. As the saying goes: *Always praise a servant displaying worth, loyalty and nobility.*

When God Vishnu arrived, Garuda explained, 'The Sea, who is very proud to be under your protection, took the chicks of my servant and brought shame on me. I have done nothing yet because I do not want anything to diminish your glory.'

'Well done,' said God Vishnu. 'Let us recover the chicks from the Sea, and go on to do business in the divine city. *They say that a master who does not punish a servant's wrongdoing earns punishment for himself.*

God Vishnu took aim with his fire-arrow at the Sea and said, 'Villain! Return the Sandpipers' chicks or else I will reduce you to dry land.'

Hearing this, the Sea took fright and gave back the chicks to the Sandpipers. Clearly, he had not assessed the strength of the birds and that of their true friends before picking a fight with them.

After Lively was persuaded to put off the fight, he asked Crafty, 'How does King Rusty fight? What is his technique?'

Crafty replied, 'Usually, he lies completely relaxed on a flat rock. If his tail is drawn in, his paws tight, his ears perked up, and he watches you closely even when you are far away, he is really ready to pounce.'

Then Crafty returned to Cautious who asked, 'So what have you achieved?'

Crafty replied, 'I have set them at odds against each other. Now, I must look out for my own interests and do it in secret just like the jackal called Clever did.'

'How was that?' asked Cautious, and Crafty told this story.

Jackal Who Tricked Lion

There was a lion named Big Roar who lived in a dark forest with his three hangers-on: Fierce the wolf, Clever the jackal, and Hump the camel. One day, Big Roar got into a fight with an angry elephant and was badly hurt. He had to go into hiding to lick his wounds while he healed. Seven days went by, and he grew thin and very hungry. So he said to his starving retinue. 'Go find a food-animal and even in my present condition I will help you kill and carve it for all of us.'

They went far and wide but could not find anything.

Clever began to plot away. 'If Hump were killed, we would have food for many days. But since Big Roar considers him a friend, he will not kill him. So I will have to trick him into doing so. After all, you can outwit anyone if you are smart.'

So he went over to Hump and said, 'I have a tip for you that could prolong Big Roar's life and be good for you too.'

'Tell me, please, and I will do as you say,' said Hump.

'Give up your body, and you will be assured of not just one but two bodies in heaven, thereby getting double the time there, and the Master can live a long life on earth.'

'OK,' said Hump, 'but Big Roar must call on the Death-God to guarantee the deal.'

Big Roar was touched by Hump's offer of sacrifice and accepted it. Hump was killed by Big Roar and torn apart by Fierce and Clever.

Then Clever got to thinking, 'Now I alone must get all the food for myself.'

Noticing that Big Roar was covered in Hump's blood, he told him to go to the river to wash up while he and Fierce guarded the food. So the lion went to the river.

When the lion was gone, Clever told Fierce, 'You are starving. Why don't you go ahead and eat? I will make your apologies when Big Roar returns.'

As soon as Fierce began to eat, Clever shouted, 'Drop it! The Master is coming.'

When Big Roar returned he saw that the camel's heart had been eaten and he lost his temper. 'Who turned our dinner into leavings? I will kill him.' Fierce looked to Clever for help, but Clever said, 'Don't look at me now. You ate the heart, didn't you?' At which point Fierce fled for his life.

Meanwhile, there came a heavily laden caravan of camels, which was taking a shortcut through the forest. The camels all had bells around their necks to warn people and animals to keep out of the way. When Big Roar heard the bells, he asked Clever to find out what the noise was. Clever pretended to go look and came back right away, saying, 'Run, Master, run. The Death-God is coming. He is angry because you brought untimely death to his camel and called upon him to be the guarantor.' So the lion also fled in fear of his life and Clever lived on the camel's meat for many days.

While Crafty was gone, Lively brooded upon his best course. 'I cannot run without being caught,' he thought. 'So I should go ahead and approach Rusty, the Lion King – after all, he might see me as a lowly subject and spare my life.' So he went up to Rusty slowly and was very troubled when he saw Rusty in the fearsome posture Crafty had forewarned him about. He sank to his knees. As they say, *the timid servant never learns when the master's purpose may change.*

Meanwhile, Rusty, seeing the bull in the position of fighting readiness that Crafty had foretold, suddenly sprang at him. Lively, though badly injured by Rusty's sharp claws, gored the lion with his horns, stepped back and stood ready to do it again.

At this point, Cautious, seeing that both were ready to kill each other, scolded Crafty: 'You stupid fool! You have done a wicked deed and made enemies of friends. You have brought trouble on the whole forest, proving that you have no idea of true governance. *One needs to always first try peaceful means and conciliation before conflict. Power without intelligence simply hastens ruin.*

Statesmanship includes five things: proper beginning; good resources, human and material; choice of time and place; preparedness for bad luck; and successful completion. But our master, King Rusty, is also at fault for trusting a false friend and counsellor like you and is paying a heavy price for doing so. He is ignorant of the ways and methods of good rulers. Remember the counsellor who got his wish? He won the king's favour and set fire to an enemy, the naked monk.'

'How did that happen?' asked Crafty, and Cautious explained with the following story.

Monk Who Left His Body Behind

There was a famous King, named Gold Throne, who dwelt in a big city. He was the overlord of small forest fiefdoms surrounding the city. One day a forest ranger came to him with the report that there was trouble brewing and the main troublemaker was Chief Poker. He needed to be controlled. So King Gold Throne called on his trusted minister, Counsellor Sage, to take care of the problem.

When the counsellor left for his task, a naked monk arrived in the city. His name was BareBack. He boasted of his astrological abilities and soon won over all the city residents as if he had bought and paid for each one!

The King became curious about the naked monk and his influence upon his people. So he asked BareBack to come to the palace. The naked monk, however, postponed his visit until the next day and when he arrived, he told the King: 'Sorry, Your Majesty, I was held up, but I had to leave my body behind last night and go to heaven where the Gods asked after you.' The King was so flattered that he stopped paying any attention to ruling or the ruled.

Counsellor Sage returned and heard the King singing the praises of the naked monk. Invited by the naked monk to see things for himself, Counsellor Sage saw BareBack go into his cabin and he saw him lock the door from the inside.

'How soon will the naked monk return?' asked the Counsellor and the King explained that the naked monk left his earthly body behind in the cabin at night and returned with another – a heavenly body – the next morning.

'If that is so,' said Counsellor Sage, 'go bring a cord of wood and burn down the cabin so that when the naked monk returns he will be able to attend the King in his heavenly body.'

'Why do you want to do this?' asked the King, and the Counsellor asked him, 'Have you ever heard the story of the girl who married a snake?'

'Tell me,' said the King, and Counsellor Sage told this story.

Girl Who Married a Snake

There was a Brahmin named Righteous who was very sad because his wife did not have any children and that made her very unhappy. He prayed and performed sacrifices on her behalf until God said to him, 'You will have the best son in the world – handsome, good and charming.'

In time, the Brahmin's wife gave birth to a snake. Other people were horrified, but she loved her son and raised him with much care.

One day, the snake's mother attended the wedding of a neighbour's son. She became sad and asked her husband Righteous to find a bride for her son.

'Who will give his daughter in marriage to a snake?' thought Righteous. Still, seeing his wife so unhappy, the Brahmin decided to search far and wide.

On his travels, he stopped at the house of a relative where he was made welcome. On his departure the next morning, the host asked the Brahmin, 'What are you searching for on your travels? Where will you go next?' On learning that Righteous was looking for a suitable bride for his son, the host immediately offered his own daughter.

When Righteous returned home with a beautiful young girl who was now engaged to his son, and her attendants, the people were shocked. Her own family members, when they learned the facts, were also unhappy. But the girl said, 'There are only three things in this world that once given, cannot be withdrawn: the word of kings, the blessing of saints and a girl given in marriage. Remember the poor parrot. *What will be, will be.*'

'How was that?' asked the people, and the girl told this story.

Parrot Named Brilliant

The God of Immortals, Indra, once owned a very intelligent and brightly coloured parrot called Brilliant. One day he was sitting on the hand of his Master when he caught a glimpse of the God of Death and backed away. The immortals surrounding God Indra were surprised and asked the Parrot, 'Why did you back away?'

'He brings harm to all living things,' the Parrot said.

So they asked the Death-God to not kill the parrot as a favour to them. But the Death-God replied, 'It is Time that decides such things.' So the immortals took the Parrot with them, went to visit Time and requested him to let the parrot live.

'It is Death who decides,' declared Time. 'Go see him.'

But when they did so, the Parrot died at the mere sight of Death. Horrified, the immortals asked, 'What is this? What happened here?'

To which the Death-God replied: 'Fate had simply

arranged that when the Parrot saw Death, he would die. It was preordained.'

*

Having told the story, the young bride-to-be married the Snake. One night, after some time had passed, she felt a man enter her room. She was terrified and about to flee when the man said to her, 'I am your husband and have left the snake's body in a chest.'

Meanwhile, Righteous woke unduly early and saw the snakeskin lying in his son's room.

'I should burn the chest and the snakeskin,' he thought, 'and then my son will not be able to return into a snake's body.' So he did burn the chest and from then on the Brahmin and his wife's son was always seen in a handsome man's body with a beautiful wife beside him.

*

After Counsellor Sage had explained his reasons for wanting to burn the cabin, the King set fire to the cabin with the naked monk's body inside.

Cautious continued to scold Crafty: 'The imposter, the naked monk, got his just deserts and you will too. Good advice is wasted upon a villain like you. As the saying goes: *You cannot teach an unteachable monkey.*'

'What do you mean?' asked Crafty, and Cautious told this story.

Unteachable Monkey

A troop of monkeys were looking to stay warm on a chilly winter evening. They found a firefly and thinking it was a spark of fire, they gathered it up carefully and put it in the middle of a bed of dry grass and leaves, and began to blow upon it. A particular Monkey blew repeatedly and vigorously on the poor firefly.

Seeing him work on his useless task, a bird named Helper, whose days were numbered, flew down from her tree and advised the Monkey to stop blowing. 'This is not fire,' she told him, 'this is a firefly.' But the Monkey paid no attention. Helper, though, kept interfering and tried again and again to make the Monkey stop what he was doing.

Finally, the Monkey exploded with rage and when she next came close, he seized her, smashed her head on a rock and killed her.

'*Advice and education are wasted* on those too stupid to learn,' continued Cautious. '*Wisdom, not beauty, and an intelligent mind are rare indeed.* Remember the son who tried to be too smart and suffocated his father?'

'How was that?' asked Crafty, and Cautious told this story. ✍

Honest and Sly

There were two young men, named Honest and Sly, who were good friends and both sons of merchants. When it became time to leave home, they decided to travel together to go seek their fortune in nearby cities.

One day, not long after they began their journey, Honest tripped over a pot that contained a thousand gold coins and appeared to have no owner. Honest, talking it over with Sly, decided to return home for he had found his fortune after all. Sly decided to come back too. When they got close to home, Honest generously offered to split his find and give half the money to his friend Sly so that they both would be welcomed back as equally successful young men.

Sly suggested they take only a hundred gold coins each with them and bury the rest as a bond to their friendship. They would always be friends because they would have this secret treasure in common. Not realizing Sly's hidden intentions, Honest agreed.

Before long, Sly – who was a spendthrift – ran out of money and requested a second installment of a hundred

gold coins each. Honest did not object. Within a few months, Sly had wasted away that money too on unnecessary things. Finally, he gave in to temptation and made a plan to steal the rest of the six hundred coins. Eventually, he took all the money and covered his tracks well in the woods.

It was not long before Sly had spent every penny of the whole fortune, gambling it away on useless things and false friends. So he came up with yet another scheme. He went to Honest and suggested it was now time to divide up the money. Honest agreed, but when they went to the spot where they had buried the pot, there was, of course, no money left. Sly began to loudly accuse Honest of stealing it. Honest became angry and suggested they carry their quarrel to court.

The judge looked for evidence or a witness to help him decide the case. At which point Sly said he had the Goddess of the Wood herself as a witness. So the judge ordered that the court would convene the next day in the wood.

Meanwhile, Sly rushed to get help from his father. He asked his father to hide in the hollow of a tree, pretend to be the Goddess of the Wood and bear false witness on his son's behalf. The father was very upset and replied, 'O Son, you have not really thought through the consequences. *Sometimes the cure is worse than the disease.* Remember the stupid herons?'

'What stupid herons?' asked Sly, and his father narrated this story.

The Cure Was Worse than the Disease

In a large fig tree in a deep dark forest near a big lake lived a pair of Herons. Whenever the Heron-Hen laid her eggs in their nest, a long black snake that lived in a hollow in the same tree would climb up and eat the chicks before they had grown wings. The Herons were devastated. One day, the mother Heron went to sit by the edge of the lake and could not stop crying.

A Crab noticed her and asked what was wrong. The mother Heron explained. 'Can you help?' she asked. But she asked the wrong creature. Herons are natural enemies of crabs, so seeing an opportunity for gain, the Crab told her to put down a trail of partly eaten fish from where the Mongoose lived in the forest to the hollow where the Snake lived. He told her that the Mongoose would eat the Snake. The mother Heron did what the Crab had advised, but the Mongoose not only

ate the Snake at the bottom of the fig tree but also the Herons up in the nest.

*

Sly however chose to ignore the warning of the story his father had told. Following his own plan, he helped his father hide in the hollow of the tree where the pot of money had been buried in the woods. When the Judge and court officers arrived the next day, they heard a voice in the tree bear witness against Honest. But, before the Judge could convict him, Honest had set a fire around the base of the tree, which in turn had suffocated Sly's father. Everyone realized that Sly had arranged a false witness, and the Judge convicted Sly, sent him to prison, and recommended Honest for a good job in the city government.

After telling Crafty the story, Cautious continued chiding him. 'You have shamed your family by destroying Lively who trusted you and in the end you are destroying our Master too. I should beware. As the saying goes: *'Where the mice eat the balance-beam, the hawk can lift an elephant, let alone a boy.'*

'What are you talking about?' asked Crafty, and Cautious told this story.

Mice That Ate Iron

There was a merchant named Prosper, who lost all his money. So he decided to leave town and go seek his fortune elsewhere. But before he left, he went to the Pawn-Broker and pawned a valuable iron balance-beam that he had inherited and which weighed a thousand kilos.

After quite a long time, Prosper returned home and went to the Pawn-Broker to reclaim his deposit, the iron balance-beam, but he was in for a surprise. 'I am afraid your balance-beam has been eaten by mice,' said the Pawn-Broker.

'Oh well,' said Prosper, 'not to worry. Nothing lasts forever. Such is life. I had better go have a bath in the river now. Would you do me a favour and send your boy with me to carry my stuff?' Feeling guilty about his own trickery, the Pawn-Broker sent his son to carry the merchant's luggage for him.

After bathing in the river, Prosper tied up the Pawn-Broker's son and forced him into the hollow of a tree.

Then he went back to the Pawn-Broker's shop and said, "I am so sorry, but a hawk carried off your son from the riverbank while I was having my bath.'

'How can that be?' shouted the Pawn-Broker in rage. 'That is impossible. You are lying!'

'Well, so how could mice eat my iron balance-beam?' said the merchant. 'Give it back and I will return your boy.'

They kept arguing and went to a nearby magistrate with their quarrel. When each told his absurd story, the magistrate laughed and ordered that they each return what he had wrongly taken. In the end, The merchant got his iron balance-beam and the Pawn-Broker got his boy back.

After telling the story, Cautious continued to berate Crafty: 'You are a knave. You could not bear Rusty's friendship with Lively. You have succeeded in destroying what you coveted. You wanted all of Rusty's favour for yourself. I don't know why I stay with you. Merely associating with you could be disastrous. As the saying goes, *even brothers can become prime examples of good and bad education.*'

'What do you mean?' asked Crafty, and Cautious told this story.

Twin Parrots, Good and Bad

A Parrot couple who lived in the woods had twins, but before they could raise the chicks, the parents died. As it happened, one baby chick was found by a Poacher and raised by him. The Poacher taught the parrot to use bad and threatening words. The other twin parrot chick was found by a wandering hermit and raised by him. The Hermit taught the parrot chick to mimic words of welcome and praise. Time passed and the Twin Parrots came to reflect their education, bad and good.

One day, a King was riding alone in the woods. He had gotten separated from his attendants and came unexpectedly upon the Poacher's hut. As he approached, the Poacher's Parrot started squawking, 'Quick. Set a trap. Tie him up. Kill him.' Hearing such threats, the King turned around and quickly rode off in another direction.

Later in the afternoon, the King reached the Hermit's hut. As he slowly, slowly, came near it, he heard another Parrot squawking. 'Welcome, welcome. Have some food. Have some cool water. Pray with us.' Upon getting such a different reception, the King began to ponder over the *differing results of associating with bad and good people.*

Having told the story, Cautious was still full of reproach. 'Just staying with you is evil,' he told Crafty. 'As they say, it is better to cling to wise foes than foolish friends. Remember the robber who died for his victims and the monkey that killed the King?'

'Remind me,' said Crafty, and Cautious told the following two stories. ✍

Sensible Foe

Once, a Prince made friends with the son of a Merchant and the son of a Professor. They soon became inseparable and spent time in all sorts of pleasurable pursuits. However, the Prince did not like riding horses or elephants, nor did he care for archery. His father, the King, decided to give him a talking-to because the Prince never engaged in royal activities.

When the Prince later told his friends about the scolding, which had made him unhappy, his friends said, 'Our fathers too keep rebuking us because we are not interested in their professions. We were enjoying our friendship and trying to ignore our problem. We see you are unhappy at home just as we are. What do you think we should do?'

The Prince replied, 'It is unmanly to stay where we are constantly scolded. Let us leave home.'

Having decided on what to do, the three friends considered how to proceed. 'Our wishes cannot be fulfilled without money,' said the Merchant's son, 'so let us go to Mineral King Mountain where we may find precious stones and make our fortunes.' So the three friends set off on their journey.

At the Mountain, as good luck would have it, they found a trove of priceless gems in brilliant colours. 'How can we guard our treasure through the forest on our way home?' they asked themselves. The Professor's son suggested that the best plan might be to swallow the gems and carry them in their stomachs. No one would even suspect them of having anything valuable with them.

So, at dinner before setting off, they swallowed the gems. But someone had been watching them the whole time. He thought, 'I too have been climbing Mineral King Mountain for many days searching for gems but without any luck. Why should the three friends get rich and not I? I will travel with these three and at nightfall, when they are asleep, I will cut open their stomachs and get the gems for myself.'

So he approached the three friends and asked, 'Would it be all right if I join you? I don't want to travel alone through the dense forest below.'

The friends agreed and the four travellers proceeded on their journey. Near the trail through the forest was a gypsy village. It wasn't a big village, but it had an Old Gypsy who kept birds that were able to foresee things most people could not. As the four travellers were passing nearby, one of the Old Gypsy's favourite birds started singing. The Old Gypsy understood the birdsong and translated it for the village chief. 'Those travellers have precious gems.'

So the Chief asked the village strongmen to catch the travellers and search them.

When they did not find anything, the Chief frisked them himself. Finding nothing valuable on them, he let them go but kept most of their clothes. However, the bird kept singing the same song, so the village Chief had them brought back and searched them one more time but in vain. The Chief was again about to let the travellers go free, when the old bird sang the same song, but this time loudly, and in great anger.

Since the bird had in the past always been correct in his prediction, the village Chief did not want to offend him, the Old Gypsy or others who respected it. He also began to suspect that the travellers may have swallowed the gems. So he announced that he would kill all four travellers the next morning to see if the gems were in their stomachs. He ordered them to be tied down for the night in a hut that served as a prison.

The three friends were silent. The captive fourth man, the thief, realized that he was a dead man. When the Chief would find the gems in the stomachs of the other three, he would certainly cut him open too. He remembered the proverb that said: *When all is lost, the noble person tries to serve others even at his own expense.* So he decided to offer to be the first one for the village Chief to cut open. By making this sacrifice, he would lose his life but might save the life and wealth of the three friends, and in so doing win himself glory in the life hereafter. The next morning the village Chief cut open the stomach of the thief and, finding nothing, he let the three friends go free.

Eventually, the Prince inherited the kingdom and became King. He made the Merchant's son the treasurer, and his other friend, the Professor's son, his Prime Minister. After delegating most of the heavy tasks of governing, the new King lived a life of ease and luxury. He acquired a pet monkey of whom he grew unduly fond. He grew to have great confidence in him and even made the Monkey his personal sword-bearer.

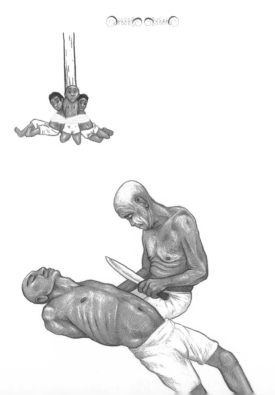

Foolish Friend

One day, the King decided to have an afternoon nap in the classical pagoda located in his ornamental gardens. As he lay down, he said to the Monkey, 'I shall rest here in this arbour. You keep careful watch and make sure no one disturbs me.' He went to sleep and the Monkey stood guard.

Soon thereafter, a honeybee arrived, drawn by the nectar in the blooming flowers, and hovered around. Then he alighted on the King's hair. The monkey tried to wave the bee away, but the bee continued his hovering and occasional sitting on the King's hair.

The Monkey got mad at the bee, drew the King's sword and swung it at the bee. He struck a hard blow that cut the King's head in two.

'So *one should beware of making friends with fools and trusting them too much,*' continued Cautious. '*It is always best to do the right thing. You have done wrong, thinking it is in your best interest.* Just you look at what is happening now.' And he pointed towards the fight before them.

Rusty and Lively, each enraged at the other, had renewed the battle. The Lion, of course, won, although Lively put up a good fight. But, having killed Lively, Rusty was filled with remorse. 'I too have done wrong. The bull was my close friend. By killing him I have only hurt myself.'

Crafty was, however, immediately at Rusty's side, ready to flatter and give false advice. 'A King is not like the common people. What is seen as a vice in the common man can be a virtue in a king.'

Cautious made one last effort to reach Rusty: '*A King should consult more than one counsellor and only then make up his mind before taking any drastic action.*' But Crafty made sure that Cautious's words were not heard. ✑

Crow, Mouse, Turtle, Deer

❧ Book Two ❧

About this Book

Book Two, here titled 'Crow, Mouse, Turtle, Deer' deals with four friends: how they meet, how they get to know each other and become friends despite being different species (one might even say, they are natural enemies), as well as how they help one another to survive and thrive when life becomes difficult.

The foundation story of the book is the account of the four friends, their past and present. The stories are narrated by Sharma, the tutor engaged by the King to wake up the minds of his three sons, the Princes, so they could learn to live and govern wisely. He tells of how a Crow named Sight first meets a Mouse named Smart and how they become friends.

Sight observes and learns from the experience of a group of doves and from Keen, the Dove King, about the effectiveness and value of cooperation and friendship. Smart was a friend of Keen and frees the ensnared doves from certain death. Sight, now appreciating the value of friendship, seeks it from Smart. In return, when fortune takes a nasty turn and they both have to flee their home city, they take refuge with Sight's friend, a turtle named Sense. The three friends then tell stories about hardship and friendship until Deer arrives and seeks their friendship.

The main or *frame* story told by Crow, Mouse, Turtle and Deer as they build their relationship is separated in this book from the *stand-alone* or *nesting* stories that are cited in the frame story.

Book Two is an elaborate tale of true friendship that flourishes despite the vastly differing natures of the individuals and the troubles they face. The strengths of each friend make the group strong and effective in addressing the challenges they face.

Crow, Mouse, Turtle, Deer

Stories	Told By	To
• Crow Observes the Doves	Sharma, Teacher	Three Princes
• Peculiar Birds	Keen, Dove King	Group of Doves
• Crow and Mouse Become Friends	Sharma, Teacher	Three Princes
• Crow and Mouse Go to See Turtle	Sharma, Teacher	Three Princes
• Mouse Loses Everything	Smart, Mouse	Sight, Crow and Sense, Turtle
• Mrs Shrewd and Her Bargain	Venerable, Holy Man	Missing Ear, Hermit
• Ill-Fated Jackal Hoarder	Brahmin	His Wife
• Man Will Get What Is Due Him	Smart, Mouse	Sight, Crow and Sense, Turtle
• Turtle Tries to Cheer up Mouse	Sharma, Teacher	Three Princes
• Weaver Named Plain	Smart, Mouse	Sense, Turtle
• Hang-Ball and Greedy Jackal	Plain, Weaver	Figure Three, Apparition
• The Deer Arrives	Sharma, Teacher	Three Princes
• Mice Set the Elephants Free	Speed, Deer	Sense, Turtle
• Deer Is Captured	Sharma, Teacher	Three Princes
• Speed Caught in a Snare	Speed, Deer	Smart, Mouse

The second set of teaching tales Sharma told was:
Crow, Mouse, Turtle, Deer.
Sharma began:

'Four friends, all poor, but having
Common sense and learning,
Lived better together than
Each could have separately.'

'What do you mean?' asked the three Princes, and
Sharma told this story.

Crow Observes the Doves

In a big banyan tree in a famous city called Sunrise lived a crow named Sight. One morning, he spied a hunter approaching his tree. The Hunter looked fearsome as he came closer, carrying his snare and his rod. Sight watched as the Hunter picked a spot, spread his net and scattered some grain. But the birds in the banyan tree who had listened to Sight's advice did not get tempted by the birdseed.

However, the leader of a flock of doves, named Keen, ignored Sight's warning. He had seen the grain beneath the tree from a long way off and brought his followers with him. As they alighted to feed, they were ensnared.

Clearly, Keen had made a big mistake. Everyone makes mistakes, but Keen kept his head. He immediately rallied his doves: 'We must all work together with one purpose. We must all fly up and carry the net with us, and we will all be saved. Remember the "one-belly–two-mouths" birds?'

'Tell us,' requested the doves, and Keen told them this story. 🖉

Peculiar Birds

By a small lake lived a couple of peculiar birds who had a common belly but two separate heads and mouths. One day, one head found some delicious berries. The second head wanted some too, so it said, 'Give me half the berries.' But the first refused to share. The second head got really angry and ate a plant that it knew was poisonous. Sure enough, since they had a common belly, they both died.

When the doves heard the story, they immediately got together, worked without fear, in complete unison, flew in a tight formation and managed to carry off the snare with them. The Hunter was amazed but figured that the doves' unity would not last long and that he would eventually get his prey. So the Hunter pursued the doves flying overhead.

Keen, however, saw the Hunter coming after them and guessed his purpose. Again, keeping his head, he directed his flock to fly over hilly areas with dense undergrowth that would be hard for the Hunter to cross.

Watching all this, Sight was surprised both by the Hunter's persistence and Keen's response. He was very impressed by how Keen was leading his doves to safety and began to follow him to see what would happen next.

Eventually, the Hunter realized that he would not be able to keep up with the flock and turned back towards his home, bemoaning the fact that he had not only lost his catch but also the snare by which he supported his family. Fate had certainly done him in.

Seeing the Hunter give up his chase, Keen directed his flock of doves to turn towards Sunrise City. His great friend, a mouse called Smart, lived there. 'He will cut through the snare and set us free,' he told his doves, egging them on.

Upon the arrival of the whole flock at his doorstep, and the noise of their wings flapping all together, Smart was quite worried. So he asked his visitors to identify themselves while he kept himself well-hidden. Once Keen had assured Smart that he was a friend in trouble, Smart welcomed him and wanted to know what happened. 'Fate has its way,' answered Keen.

When Smart began to cut through the net nearest to him, Keen objected and said, 'Please cut the bonds of my followers first. As the saying goes, *the King who honours his retainers more than is their due always has followers even when his wealth is lost.* Besides, if something goes wrong and your teeth begin to hurt, I would lose everything seeing my attendants suffering and would go to hell.' Smart cut the bonds of all the doves and they were free to fly home.

That is why they say that a man can make gains with the help of friends even when the going gets difficult. So make friends and think of them as a treasure. ✍

Crow and Mouse Become Friends

Sight understood what Smart had really been saying. 'Goodness, this is one intelligent mouse,' he thought. 'Perhaps I should try and make friends with him? Even though I am naturally suspicious, I should learn to trust others for they do say that *even those who are self-sufficient should seek friends who can be invaluable*.'

Having thought things through, Sight approached the entrance to Smart's home. Smart had the equivalent of a rabbit's warren or a mole's burrow, with several interconnected underground tunnels. It had many entrances and many exits so that, if in danger, Smart and his followers could enter and leave in several ways and would not be an easy catch.

Sight called out, 'Smart, please come out.'

Staying hidden, Smart asked, 'Who is it?'

'My name is Sight,' replied Sight. 'I am a crow.'

Immediately Smart became concerned. His visitor was of a species hostile to mice, so he said, 'Please leave immediately!' But the Crow was persistent.

'I come in good faith,' the Crow said. 'Please talk to me for a while.'

'I see no good coming from talking to you,' Smart said.

In answer the Crow explained that he had seen how bright and competent Smart was and how he had readily freed the doves. 'There may come a day,' said Sight, 'when I could also be caught like your friend Keen, and I would need a friend like you. Please let us be friends, even if we are different and seen as natural enemies.'

But Smart still hesitated. 'You eat and I am your food. How can I trust you enough to be friends? After all,' he continued, '*a friendship between those who are not equals never works. Ordinary enemies can be dealt with, but natural enemies are lifelong. Think of the hostility between snakes and mongooses, dogs and cats, lions and elephants, crows and owls, herbivores and carnivores, gods and devils, scholars and idiots, saints and sinners. . .*

'But,' the Crow cried, 'this doesn't make sense, does it? *A man becomes a friend for a reason and grows hostile for a reason. So the prudent make friends, not foes. Don't give cause for making a foe.*'

So the discussion on friendship and moral principles continued between the Crow and the Mouse. In the end, each was convinced of the intelligence and common sense of the other, each had won the confidence of the other and each decided to give friendship between creatures of a different kind, such as they were, a chance.

Sight then resumed his search for food. He flew over a nearby forest and came upon the remains of a buffalo killed by a tiger. He not only ate his fill but took some choice pieces to give his newfound friend, Smart. When he presented the meat to the Mouse, he found that his friend had also been gathering corn and rice to share with the Crow. The two were very pleased with the gifts given and received. *As they say, friendship grows by doing six things: receiving, giving, listening, talking, dining and entertaining.* By doing these the Crow and the Mouse became fast friends.

Crow and Mouse Go to See Turtle

Time passed. One day, when a long-lasting drought gripped the countryside, and famine could be seen round the corner, Sight became very sad and said to Smart: 'Things are getting really bad. People are starving and instead of putting birdseed out in their yards, they are setting traps to catch birds for food. I haven't been caught yet but could be next. So I have decided to leave this area.'

'Where will you go?' asked Smart.

Sight replied, 'To the far west is a great lake surrounded by dense woods. My dear friend Sense, a turtle, lives there. He will feed me fish and we will enjoy good fellowship with interesting conversation and cheer, and I will be able to forget the disaster spreading here.'

'Given the current situation, I will follow you because I too have a great sorrow.'

'What is it?' asked Sight, but Smart simply said, 'It is a long story. I will tell you when we reach where we are going.'

'We really should travel together, but I travel by air and you on the ground,' pointed out Sight. 'Perhaps you should ride on me?'

'Please carry me gently,' requested Smart.

'I know all eight kinds of flight,' replied Sight. 'A long steady cruise, an upward dart, a smooth horizontal, a sharp downward, a straight rise, a clear circling, a defined zigzag and a short flight. Not to worry, I will get you to our destination in comfort.'

When Sense saw them as they reached the lake, he wondered at the strange bedfellows. When he understood who his visitors were, he welcomed them.

As they sat down to dinner after the usual pleasantries, Sense asked, 'Who is this mouse?' Sight explained that Smart was his very dear friend whose virtues were too numerous to count but that great grief had brought him to Sense.

'Pray, tell us the story of your great sadness,' asked Sense and Smart began the story of his great loss. 🖎

Mouse Loses Everything

Mouse began his story: 'You have heard of a city called Sunrise. I used to live there in a hermit's cell. The Hermit, called Missing Ear – for he had lost it in an accident early on – used to beg for alms. When he got home, he would eat his fill of the best food he had been given and leave some for his servant in the begging bowl, which he used to hang on a peg. I could always reach the bowl no matter how high he hung it and I lived quite well on it.

'One day, the Hermit had a visitor, a holy man named Venerable. Missing Ear paid him due deference and welcomed him in. As the guest sat recounting a particularly worthy tale, Missing Ear had to get up quite often to tap the begging bowl to keep me from eating all the food in it. Annoyed at the interruptions, Venerable decided to leave and go where he was more welcome. He rightly pointed out that a true friend always gives full attention and listens wholeheartedly. "You are not really listening to me," said Venerable. "You are a lonely hermit and still have too much pride. I am leaving."

'Missing Ear was upset. "Please, please don't leave. I only *seem* inattentive for I must keep tapping on the begging bowl to keep the mouse from eating all the food I have saved. This mouse is really very clever and I have to be ever vigilant. He seems to best me no matter what I try to do to keep the food safe."

"'Have you found the mouse hole?" asked Venerable.

"'No," was the reply.

"'Surely," continued the holy man, "the mouse hole entrance must be over his hoard. And it must be the smell from it that makes the mouse so clever and frisky. The smell of wealth and its enjoyment increases with the hoard. But there must be a reason why this mouse can always outwit you. As they say, if Mrs Shrewd was bargaining hulled grains for un-hulled ones, she must have had a good reason."'

'How was that?' asked Missing Ear, and Venerable told this story. ✑

Mrs Shrewd and Her Bargain

Once, Venerable needed a place to stay in the rainy season and asked a Brahmin for help. The Brahmin gave him shelter and Venerable lived there for a while, continuing to perform his pious duties. One day he woke early and overheard the Brahmin say to his Wife: 'Tomorrow is the winter solstice, a big day for us, so I will go to a different village to get donations. Please give any Brahmin who comes to our door looking for alms as much food as you can in honour of the Sun.'

'But,' the Wife retorted, 'how can I donate food when we have so little for ourselves? Why should I feed any beggar?'

The Brahmin was upset. 'You know the saying: *Even if you only have a mouthful, give half to the needy. The reward in heaven is as much as if you gave away half of untold riches.* Remember, the greedy jackal killed by the bow?'

'No,' said his Wife, and the Brahmin told this story.

Ill-fated Jackal Hoarder

A hunter set out to hunt in a forest. He soon saw a boar and quickly drew his arrow and shot him. But the boar managed to gore the hunter in the stomach so that both died in pain. Later that same day, a hungry Jackal came by and saw the unexpected kill. Realizing his good luck, he decided to feast on it very slowly so as to sustain himself for many days. He would carefully hoard his find. As the saying goes, *wise men sip fine drink to savour it to the fullest.* So the Jackal, with apparent good foresight, began with the sinew attached to the bow. The gut string broke

when stretched too far and snapped back hard so that the bow-tip pierced through the roof of his mouth into his head. He died from the pain.

'The point is,' continued the Brahmin, '*five things are preordained before birth: the length of life, fate, wealth, learning and the tomb.*'

'All right,' the Wife replied. 'I have some sesame grain left that I will grind up into flour so I can feed any Brahmin who comes to our door.' Hearing his wife promise to do the right thing, the Brahmin left as planned for a nearby village to get donations.

The Wife, known as Mrs Shrewd, proceeded to soften the sesame grains in boiling water, hulled them, put them in a dish and kept them out in the hot sun, and went about doing her other chores. A stray dog came by house and started eating from the dish.

'Oh dear,' said the Wife to herself, '*when fate turns against us, it cannot be stopped.* The sesame grains are no longer fit to eat. What shall I do? Perhaps I will take them to a neighbour's house and offer to exchange un-hulled sesame for hulled. Anyone will like such a deal.'

'As it happened,' Venerable continued, 'Mrs Shrewd went to a house where I was a guest. There, the housewife, of course, agreed to her offer, but when her husband came home and she told him about it, he immediately told her to throw the hulled sesame away. 'Mrs Shrewd is too astute to give anything away without profit,' he said. 'She must have had a reason for such a deal.'

'Likewise, let us see if we can figure out why the Mouse always gets the food in your begging bowl,' said Venerable. 'Do you have a digging tool?'

'I have a pick-axe,' said Missing Ear. 'Let's wake up early in the morning and follow the mouse's tracks to his hoard.

Smart was very upset when he heard these words. 'This will spell complete ruin for me. This holy man, Venerable, is one brainy Brahmin. He will find my stash of riches for sure.'

So he quickly changed course and ran off with his followers to a new hole. But fate was against him and Venerable was able to find everything he was looking for with the help of a pick-axe and the neighbour's cat.

'Between them,' Smart went on, 'they destroyed my home and my food stores, scared off my followers and stole my riches. I left, alone and dejected. My vigour had been sustained by my sense of well-being and the knowledge that I was wealthy. Without it, I was but a poor mouse without a following. As the saying goes, *when a man is bowed down by poverty and an unkind fate, his friends turn to foes, and love to hate. Beggary is as bad as death itself.* What course is still open to me? *Living by stealing or robbing is accursed as is living always on another's charity.*

'So, after a long time, I decided to try and reclaim my property even if I died in the attempt. My effort failed, but I escaped death because my time was not up yet. Predestination, as always, played its part. That is why they say: *A man will get his due and even the Gods cannot prevent it.*'

'How can that be?' asked the Crow and the Turtle, and the Mouse told this story. ✍

Man Will Get What Is Due Him

There was a trader named Money whose son lived at home. One day, the Son bought a book that had only one line written in it: 'Man will get what is due him.' The Father asked his Son, 'How much did you pay for this?'

'A hundred silver coins,' replied the Son.

The Father, Money, became enraged at his son's inability to grasp the value of silver coins. 'How can you ever make a living if you spend without considering the return!' he told the Son. 'You had better leave and try earning your keep.'

The Son had no choice but to go far away from home. He took his book with him and became obsessed with what was written in it. So much so that when anyone in the city where he finally ended up asked him something he always replied with, 'Man will get what is due him.' So he got the nickname, Payback.

Meanwhile, it so happened that a Princess named Moonlight was taking a stroll in the park with a girlfriend and saw a Prince riding by. She was instantly smitten and asked her friend to arrange an introduction and meeting. The Girlfriend approached the Prince and told him that the Princess Moonlight had fallen in love with him and that he should visit her. 'You can climb up to the Princess' balcony using the ladder that I will place nearby for you.' The Prince agreed and left.

By nightfall, however, the Prince decided not to go for the secret visit. It would not be honourable to sneak off at night to meet a Princess. However, as it happened, Payback came by on his nightly wanderings, noticed the ladder and climbed up to the balcony. Princess Moonlight, convinced that he was the right man, treated him with affection, respect and great generosity. 'You are definitely the love of my life,' she said. 'I will never have another. Now I have told you everything about myself. Why don't you talk to me?'

'Man will get what is due him.' He replied. Stunned by Payback's response, the Princess quickly sent him away.

Payback walked to a derelict temple building and went to sleep in a corner on the floor. Soon, a policeman showed up to meet someone secretly. When the Policeman saw Payback, he asked 'Who are you?' to which Payback replied with his usual 'Man will get what is due him'.

The Policeman was shocked to hear such words and guiltily suggested that Payback go to his house and sleep in his bed. Payback, of course, accepted the generous offer.

Next day, as Payback walked along a brightly lit city street, he met a young man on his way to get married and he joined in the procession of friends and relatives. They soon reached the bride's house all decked out with party tents and wedding decorations. Just then a rogue elephant appeared and ran amuck, destroying everything in sight. The guests fled, even the bridegroom. Payback saw the terrified bride hide in a corner and ran to her help. Somehow he managed to protect her from the elephant, who took off soon enough.

When everyone came back, they saw the bride-to-be in Payback's arms. The bridegroom confronted her father in anger: 'First you promised your daughter to me and then handed her to another man!'

The Father turned to his daughter, saying, 'What is the meaning of this?' and she replied, 'This man saved my life. I will not have another man hold my hand as long as I live.'

Everyone who heard her words was taken

with the story and quickly told everyone else. By mid-morning, the Princess Moonlight, the Policeman, and even the King arrived on the scene where a great crowd was now gathered.

'What is going on?' the King asked Payback. 'Speak without fear.'

'Man will get what is due him,' replied Payback. Hearing the words again, the Princess said, 'No one can break this law. Not even the gods.' Then the bride said, 'No one should take what is mine.'

The King eventually arrived at the truth by piecing together the various accounts of everyone involved. He was rather impressed by Payback, gave him his own daughter in marriage and made him the Crown Prince since he did not have a son of his own. Everybody lived happily thereafter.

After the Mouse finished telling the story, he went on: 'I learned a lot from Payback. He truly believed that most people do get their just deserts, but I also recovered from my own money madness. I had forgotten that my hoard of gold wasn't the only thing I had lost. I had also lost contentment. Anyway', he concluded, 'it was at this time of my great sorrow that Sight needed my help. And when Sight decided to visit you, Sense, I too tagged along although I am still upset about leaving my home and country.'

Turtle Tries to Cheer up Mouse

'Don't lose heart, my dear fellow,' said Sense. '*You are intelligent and with wise action you can make any country your own just as the lion makes any forest his kingdom. We must always be energetic because man and beast, friends, and even money are drawn to vigour. Competence is at home with the brave and the sturdy because they live an active life. There is no difference between a native and foreign country for those who are competent and competitive.* Smart, today your purse may be light, but with your brains and energy and determination, you can fill it up again. *The intelligent man enjoys his money by spending it wisely, or giving it away to the needy. Only the miser hoards it and so may as well not have it.* Always remember, *there is no treasure like charity, no wealth like contentment, no gem like character and no wish like health.* You are still rich. But remember also that *some are born to enjoy the pleasures that money provides, but some are born merely to save it.* Think of the simple Weaver.'

'Tell me,' requested Smart, and Sense told him this story. ✐

Weaver Named Plain

There was once a Weaver named Plain who lived in a large city with his wife. He wove beautiful fabrics that people made into clothes, which were prized by many. He worked hard, but never seemed to earn more than a modest living. Yet he saw others who were not as good as he was at weaving but made lots of money.

Plain got increasingly discouraged and dissatisfied until one day he announced to his wife that he was going to another city.

'My dear,' the Wife said, 'you are making a mistake. Money doesn't come to people who travel! What fate has willed always follows. The Doer and the Deed are as intertwined as sunlight and shade, no matter where you are.'

But Plain disagreed. 'A deed only happens with effort. I must leave from here.' So he went to Expanding City and worked there for three years. His work sold better and when he had saved three hundred gold coins, he decided to return home.

On his way back he had to cross fairly dense woods. To be safe, he climbed a tall banyan tree at sunset and went to sleep. He was woken by two shrouded human figures arguing with each other.

Figure One said, 'Doer, you know you must prevent Plain from ever having more than a modest living. Why did you allow him to get three hundred gold coins?'

Figure Two replied, 'Listen, Deed, I must reward enterprise, so I had to let him have the money. What happens next is your problem. You can take it away.'

Hearing them, Plain quickly checked his purse and found it empty. He was truly dejected because his hard-earned money had disappeared in a flash and he could not face going home to his wife empty-handed. So he went back to Expanding City. There he worked doubly hard and managed to save five hundred gold coins in just one year. He started for home again, but by a different route.

At sunset, he found himself under the same banyan tree as before and was very upset. But he climbed up again with his money purse and went to sleep. Again, he awoke to the same two Figures arguing.

Figure One said, 'Doer, why did you give Plain five hundred gold coins? He is not supposed to have more than a modest living.'

Again, Figure Two replied, 'Deed, I have to give to the enterprising. The final consequence is your affair. Why blame me?'

Again, Plain looked in his money purse and found it empty. He couldn't bear it any longer and decided to hang himself from the branch of the accursed banyan tree. However, just when he was about to hang, a third figure appeared and said, 'Don't be so hasty. I am the one who takes your money and do not allow you more than a modest living. Just go home. But because you have touched me, I will grant you one wish.'

'Just make me rich,' requested Plain.

'What on earth will you do with money you cannot enjoy or give away for you are to have no use of it except for living modestly?' asked Figure Three.

'I want it even if I can't use it,' answered Plain. 'Think of the greedy jackal.'

'How was that?' asked Figure Three and Plain told this story.

Hang-ball and the Greedy Jackal

In a small town near some woods there lived a very virile young bull nicknamed Hang-ball because of his very large and very prominent testicles. One day, a female jackal named Nagger thought they would taste good. She believed they would fall down soon enough of their own accord and so forced her husband to follow the bull around.

The Jackal, named Easy Led, thought it was a fool's errand. 'I would rather not go after the bull in the hope of getting a treat. I think it is much better if we stay here

with the surety of catching mice regularly for our dinner.'

But greedy Nagger insisted. 'Perseverance will pay off,' she said.

Easy Led followed the bull for fifteen long years, egged on by his wife. In the end, both had to admit it was time to give up.

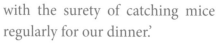

Having told the story, Plain explained, 'If I am rich, I will become an object of desire.'

Still, Figure Three hesitated. 'Go back to Expanding City,' he said, 'and observe closely two sons of merchants, named Penny-Hide and Penny-Fling. After you have done so, you may ask for the nature of one or the other.' Saying this, Figure Three disappeared.

Back went Plain to Expanding City and searched out Penny-Hide's house. When he arrived there, he sat down in the courtyard to see what would happen. He was given a meagre meal and no kindness, and had to sleep on an uncomfortable cot out of doors.

In the middle of the night, he heard the same two figures that had appeared before.

Figure One asked, 'Doer, why are you making more expense for Penny-Hide by making him feed Plain?'

'Deed, you cannot blame me,' the other figure said. 'I have to account for earnings and expenses. The final result is your affair.'

Plain left Penny-Hide's home, hungry, and went to Penny-Fling's the next morning. He was welcomed warmly and given not just food but also clothing and a comfortable bed. That night Plain again saw the figures and listened in.

'Doer,' Figure One said, 'Penny-Fling has just gotten himself deeper into debt by being so hospitable to Plain.'

'Deed', said Figure Two, 'I had to do it. The final consequence is your affair.'

At dawn the next day, a policeman showed up with money by the King's favour and gave it to Penny-Fling. Plain pondered upon what he had observed and when Figure Three appeared, he asked to be made a person like Penny-Fling who enjoyed and shared his money even when it was little. ✍

'So there is little point in spending time in worry and woe, for fate will decide good or bad for me and you,' continued Sense. '*There is no penance like patience, no peace like contentment, no pleasure like sharing, no joy like mercy and no meaning like friends.* But enough of preaching. Please stay here in friendship with me as long as you like.'

Sight also joined in the conversation, adding, 'You are so right, Sense, so wise. As they say, *what good is manhood that doesn't make the sorrowful secure, what good is wealth that doesn't help the poor, what good is an action that doesn't result in betterment and what good is a life that doesn't bring approval.*' ✑

The Deer Arrives

Just then a deer named Speed arrived at the lakeshore where the three friends were talking. He was panting with thirst and trembling from fear. Immediately, the three friends made themselves scarce: Sight flew up into a tree, Smart went into a hole in the ground, Sense dived into the lake.

After a while, Sight flew off to scout for any lurking danger and finding no sign of it, came back to reassure his friends. 'All is quiet,' he announced. 'The deer just came to the lake for water.'

So all three friends gathered as before and invited the deer to join them. Speed thought things through: 'The turtle can't hurt me out of the water, and the mouse and crow eat only carrion.' So he joined them.

Sense asked, 'What brings you here?'

'I am tired of a life without love,' replied Speed. 'I have been hounded most of my life by hunters and their dogs, and it is only fear that gives me the speed to outrun them.

So I came to this place looking for water and hoping to find friendship.'

Sense said, 'We are small and you are big. It is unnatural for us to be friends. We would never be able to do you any favours.'

'Why are you selling yourself short?' said Speed. 'Remember the mice that set the elephants free?'

'How was that?' asked Sense, and Speed told this story.

Mice Set the Elephants Free

Once there was an old city that became so rundown that people left it. Soon afterwards it turned into a colony of mice, where they began to live and thrive.

Time passed and the mice multiplied manifold. One day an Elephant-King came that way with his very large herd. As the elephants tramped through Mouse City on their way to a lake where there was plenty of water, they destroyed everything in their path and killed many of the mice. When they had gone, the surviving mice gathered to figure out a way to prevent such carnage happening ever again, for they worried that if the elephants came that way again, their entire race would be extinguished.

The mice eventually decided that the best way to proceed would be to go to the lake and negotiate a truce with the elephants. When they appeared before the Elephant-King, they bowed low and respectfully petitioned him: 'O King, we have suffered such destruction at the hands of your followers that we fear extinction if you pass through our city again. So we come here to beg for your mercy and request that you travel by a different route in the future. Please consider that even animals as small as mice may be of some service to you in the future.'

The Elephant-King thought the mice's request was entirely reasonable and granted it.

More time passed and it came to be that the king of a nearby region ordered his soldiers to trap elephants for their ivory. Eventually, they trapped the Elephant-King and many in his herd. When he was all bound up, the Elephant-King brooded upon how he could escape from the trap of certain death. Then he remembered the mice and realized that only they could help him now. So he somehow managed to get a baby elephant to take his message to the mice with information on where they were being held. When the mice learned that they were needed to free the elephants, they gathered in the thousands and gnawed through the ropes, repaying their debt.

When Sense heard the story, he said, 'We will be happy to make friends with you. Please stay here by this lake with us and think of it as your own home.' So Speed joined in and the four friends lived together and talked day and night about religion, ethics, economics and many other important subjects. ✍

Deer Is Captured

One day, Speed did not appear at their usual meeting place. The three friends began to worry almost immediately and their fear only grew. They became convinced that Speed was in trouble.

Sense and Smart said to Sight, 'You are the only one who can help in this emergency. Would you please fly up high and see what could have happened to Speed? And please return as soon as you are able to with some news.'

So Sight soared up and flew in widening circles to see if he could find Speed. Quite soon he saw him caught in a strong deer trap made with thick ropes and braced with wood. When he alighted nearby, he asked Speed, 'How did you get caught in this trap?'

But Speed responded with, 'There is no time for that. You make me happy just by your presence. *To have a friend when the end is near is itself a great boon.* Please forgive the impatience I showed in our discussions and, likewise, ask Sense and Smart to pardon me. Let only the memory of our friendship live.'

To which Sight said, 'Feel no fear, Speed, while you have friends like us in your hour of need. I will return as soon as I can with Smart to gnaw through your bonds.'

Then Sight flew back to the lake as fast as could and returned with Smart on his back. When the Mouse saw the Deer in captivity, he too asked, 'My friend, you are always cautious and have a shrewd eye, so how did you get caught?'

And Speed said, 'Why ask? Fate does what it will. Who can fight an unseen enemy? Please quickly cut my bonds before the merciless hunter returns.'

'Not to worry,' said Smart, 'I will start gnawing right away. But do tell me how you got caught for I might learn from your story.'

'OK, if you insist,' said Speed. 'This is the second time I have been been captured.'

'Tell me the story of the first time,' requested Smart. So Speed told the story about his first captivity. ✍

Speed Caught in a Snare

'When I was six months old I used to run ahead of my herd in high spirits to show how fast I was. That is why I got the name Speed. I did not, however, know both the ways that deer run: straight, and leaping. One day I lost sight of my herd, got really scared and ran straight as fast as I could in the direction I thought the herd had gone. I didn't see the snare in front of me and got caught. The herd had seen it and simply leapt over it. I was too young and did not know how to leap properly. So I was captured.

'When the hunter came back and saw that I was still a fawn, he took pity on me. He took me home to give me as a pet to a young prince. The Prince treated me with great affection and I quickly became the court plaything, passed from one to another, which I really did not like. Finally, when the rainy season was at its height, I cried out loudly in longing for my family.

'The poor Prince thought he had somehow been bewitched, for how could a deer say something in a language he could understand. He was so worried that he stopped eating and developed a fever, and put all the blame on me. The courtiers took it out on me, beating me up as often as they could. I survived because my time was not yet up and a court priest helped me. He explained to the Prince that all animals talk but not aloud in front of humans.

'"You should not be afraid of the fawn," he said. "He simply misses his family."

'So the Prince ordered his servants to take me back to the forest and set me free, and he quickly recovered from his illness.

'That is the story of my first captivity and here I am ensnared again for *there is no avoiding fate*', said Speed.

At this point Sense joined them. He was so concerned about his friend Speed whom he had followed even though the going had been very hard. Seeing Sense arrive, the others were even more distressed.

Smart spoke for all of them when he said, 'You should not have come. You will not be able to save yourself when the bonds are cut and the hunter is near. Speed will run away fast, leaping and bounding. Sight will fly up into a tree and even I will find a hole to slide into. What will you do when the hunter returns, which will be very shortly?'

To which Sense simply replied, *'It is better to lose your life than your friends.'*

Of course, the hunter arrived just then and Smart's fears were realized. Bonds cut, Speed bounded off. He didn't see Smart and Sight who did exactly as Smart had predicted. Only Sense, the slow turtle, remained visible. The hunter, resigned to the loss of the deer, grabbed the turtle, tied his feet, slung it over a stick and carried him off.

When Smart saw what was happening, he bemoaned his fate: 'First came loss of property, then my followers –

my own kind – fled from me, then I had to leave home and country, and now fate is planning to take away my friend. Ah, the loss of my friend will be the death of me.' By then Sight and Speed reached Smart and added their lament to his.

A few minutes had passed when Smart had an idea and said to the others, 'We might still have a chance of saving Sense. Speed, get to that pond there and play dead. Sight, you jump up and down on Speed's head and pretend to be plucking his eyes and make as loud a squawking sound as you can make. The hunter will turn back to look and be sure to think Speed is dead. He will be drawn back immediately by his greed, getting such a big catch without any effort. He will put Sense down on the ground while he goes for Deer and I will quickly gnaw at Turtle's ropes and free him so he can get to the pond before the hunter knows what is happening. Speed, the minute you hear the splash, jump up and run for your life. Sight, you fly off, and I will seek a hole.'

The friends quickly and carefully carried out their plan. They all became quite invisible and to the hunter it seemed a conjurer's trick. Suddenly, he became afraid for his own life and left the woods as fast as he could, empty-handed.

That is how the four friends got a new lease of life and they lived together in friendship for many, many years. ☙

Crows and Owls

About this Book

Book Three, here titled 'Crows and Owls', is about how to deal with conflict when the stakes are high, how to prevent enemies from growing too strong and how to consider an array of strategies when faced with strong enemies: from working towards peace, going to war (if necessary), retreating, standing your ground regardless of the consequences, making alliances or deceiving your enemies.

The main lessons: never trust an enemy. Above all, be cautious and always on your guard. Learn the dangers of foolish decisions, failure to keep secrets, betrayal, corruption, deceit and stupidity. Prudence in dealing with enemies and one's own counsellors is more important than valour. One must discern the dangers and advantages of conciliation, the risk and rewards of self-sacrifice, and the difference between true and false friends. One must also know the critical importance of planning and the courtesy due to, as well as the special danger of, an enemy who comes as a supplicant.

The *frame* story describes the lifelong enmity between Crows and Owls, how it arose and how the Owls got stronger without any action on the part of the Crows. Eventually the Crows decide to fight back. Both the Crow King and the Owl King consult trusted counsellors who give them advice on how to proceed. This advice is illustrated through tales that form most of the book's *stand-alone* and *nesting* stories. These are separated in this presentation from the main or frame story about the struggle between Crows and Owls by a simple method: the white pages of the book contain the nesting stories and the coloured pages carry the main or frame story of the Crow-Owl conflict. This allows the reader to choose how they want to read the book: frame story only, selected stand-alone stories, or sequentially.

Meanwhile, the frame story of the two adversaries continues on the coloured pages and can be read without interruption of the nesting stories. The book can be read in its entirety to experience the original design of this book of stories.

Crows and Owls

Stories	Told By	To
• Crows and Owls	Sharma, Teacher	Three Princes
• Birds Pick a King	Live-Strong, Crow	Spirit, Crow-King
• How the Rabbit Fooled the Elephant	Crow	Group of Birds
• Umpire Cat and His Ruling	Crow	Group of Birds
• How the Brahmin Lost His Goat	Live-Strong, Crow	Spirit, Crow-King
• How the Angry Ants Ate the Giant Snake	Live-Strong, Crow	Spirit, Crow-King
• Snake Who Paid in Gold	Red-Eye, Owl	Owl-King
• Unfriendly Swans of Lotus Lake	Brahmin	His family
• Doves' Sacrifice	Fierce-Eye, Owl	Owl-King
• Old Man Who Had a Young Wife	Flame-Eye, Owl	Owl-King
• Brahmin, Thief, and Demon Ghost	Flame-Eye, Owl	Owl-King
• Snake in the Prince's Belly	Wall-Eye, Owl	Owl-King
• Carpenter, Duped by a Wicked Wife	Red-Eye, Owl	Group of Counsellors
• Once a Mouse, Always a Mouse	Red-Eye, Owl	Live-Strong, Crow
• Bird with Gold Droppings	Red-Eye, Owl	Counsellor, Owl
• Talking Cave	Red-Eye, Owl	His Staff
• Frogs That Rode Snake-back	Live-Strong, Crow	Spirit, Crow-King
• Brahmin's Revenge	Fang, Snake	Another Snake

The third set of teaching tales Sharma told was:
Crows and Owls.
 Sharma began:

 'Even if you are reconciled,
 Never trust an enemy;
 The Owls had their cave burned
 When fire-wielding Crows arrived.'

 'How come?' asked the three Princes, and Sharma told this story.

Crows and Owls

There was once a large city called Earth Valley surrounded by hills. At one edge of the city, there was a sprawling banyan tree. In its dense branches lived a colony of crows and their King named Spirit. Not far away, in a cave, lived a rival King, a great owl named Valour, who held a lifelong grudge against crows. Whenever he met a crow, he would kill him. He had killed so many over the years that there was a ring of crow skeletons around the trunk of the banyan tree.

Eventually, the crows realized they had to do something. *They had allowed an enemy to progress without taking any action to stop it.* So King Spirit summoned his counsellors and said: 'Our enemy is proud and vigorous, and attacks at night when he can see and we cannot. We can't counter-attack in the day because we don't know where his fortress is located. *There are six ways of proceeding: try to negotiate peace, go to war, retreat by changing our base, take a stand regardless of the consequences, make alliances with others if possible, or try*

duplicity by sowing discord in enemy ranks. What do you advise we do?'

King Spirit had five learned and trustworthy ministers of long standing: Live-Again, Live-Well, Live-Along, Live-On and Live-Long. Each gave his advice and each recommended a different course of action.

'*One should not go to war with a powerful enemy,*' said Live-Again. '*Make peace instead.*'

'I disagree,' said Live-Well. '*This enemy is cruel, greedy and without principles. You should fight him.* If you try to make peace, he will continue his piecemeal violence. *He may seem the stronger, but the small often slay the bigger with determination and energy.*'

When asked for his advice, Live-Along disagreed with both Live-Again and Live-Well. '*The enemy is strong and vicious, so you should neither make peace nor wage war. Change your base position.*'

Then King Spirit turned to Live-On, who said, 'I disapprove of peace, war and especially a change of base. *A crocodile can beat an elephant, but away from his natural habitat he is at a total loss. Stay entrenched at home, stand firmly resolved to do or die.* That is where glory lies.'

Live-Long had yet another recommendation. '*Seek an alliance with another group for there is strength in numbers even if each is not strong by himself.*'

Having heard each counsellor out, King Spirit then turned to a very wise old retainer named Live-Strong who had advised his father too.

'Sir, I asked you to sit in our strategy session so you could hear my counsellors' advice. Now I ask you to guide me.'

Live-Strong took his time before replying respectfully, 'Your Majesty, while all the proposals thus far have merit, the present situation requires duplicity. You *cannot afford to be truthful and open with an enemy, even a former enemy, or a false friend. You must always be vigilant for a vulnerable side of the enemy.*'

'But how can I discover his vulnerability if I do not even know where he lives?' asked King Spirit.

Then Live-Strong told him how to *spy on a foe through his functionaries to whom important duties have been delegated. One engages spies to sow intrigue and discord among important groups like counsellors, commanders, princes and the like. But one must also be wary of people like the royal household, the courtiers, the chamberlain, and various types of purveyors in one's own camp who can be easily corrupted.*'

'Sir,' asked King Spirit, 'how ever did the deadly feud between crows and owls start?' and Live-Strong told this story. 🙶

Birds Pick a King

Once upon a time, all kinds of birds gathered together: swans, cranes, herons, doves, pigeons, partridges, swallows, sparrows, cuckoos, woodpeckers, peacocks, parrots, cardinals, blue jays, goldfinches, skylarks, sandpipers, eagles, falcons, vultures, penguins, pelicans, owls and many, many others. They came together because they were concerned about not having a King Protector. They said, 'We have always thought of Garuda as our King, but he is really God Vishnu's bird and serves him first and pays little attention to us. We need a Bird-King Protector who will defend us properly.'

During this discussion, many of the birds noticed a wise old owl sitting quietly among them and, without thinking things through, asked him to be their king. They then proceeded to make the arrangements for a very grand coronation.

When everything was just about ready, the owl was all decked out in royal robes and sat upon a handsome throne, awaiting the ceremony to begin. Just then a large

black crow flew in with a very loud squawk and alighted right in the middle of the podium. When the other birds saw him, they whispered to each other, 'The crow is the shrewdest among all birds. Let us ask him his opinion on what we are about to do.'

So they said to the Crow, 'You know, the birds have no King Protector. So we unanimously decided to ask the owl to be our king and are about to crown him. What do you think?'

The Crow laughed. 'That is foolish. He is mean, looks ugly and is blind in the daytime. Why would birds who see in the day want a king who can only see at night? Besides, Garuda is our king. A second king is not a good idea. After all, Garuda's very name keeps birds safe up to a point because everyone knows he serves God Vishnu himself and, therefore, has powerful friends. Remember, even feigning a message from the Moon helped the rabbits live in comfort.'

'How so?' asked the birds, and the Crow told them this story.

How the Rabbit Fooled the Elephant

There was an Elephant-King who had four tusks and ruled over a very large herd of elephants. One time, during a twelve-year drought, all the tanks, ponds, swamps and lakes in his area began to dry up.

The poor elephants said to him, 'O King, our children are thirsty and some are even near death. Help us find water.' So the Elephant-King sent scouts far and wide and in all directions to search for water. They eventually found a lovely crater lake, the Lake of the Moon, with clear blue water, which all creatures that lived near it enjoyed. It was full of water dwellers, but its shore also supported many, many animals from small ones to big ones, including a colony of rabbits. The elephant scouts hurried back to tell the Elephant-King about their find.

As soon as he heard about the lake, the King left to get to it as fast as he could with his large and lumbering herd. When they reached the shore of the Lake of the Moon, the elephants plunged right in, creating havoc along the edge of the lake. Once they had their fill, they returned home until it was time to get to the water again.

Unfortunately, the elephants destroyed more than just the lakeshore. They had also destroyed the warrens of the rabbit colony that had existed on that lakeshore for a long time. Many rabbits were killed in the stampede. The surviving rabbits gathered together to figure out what to do. The Rabbit-King asked for the help of his most respected counsellor named Victory, who had served him well for many years.

'I cannot go myself,' said the King, 'but I want you to go as my emissary. You know all the facts. Speak with respect as if you were me speaking. Make the best arguments that will help save us from further calamity.'

So Victory left and saw that the Elephant-King had already started on the return journey to the Lake of the Moon. He seemed invincible surrounded by his strong retinue of elephants. Victory climbed up a high and scraggly pile of rocks and from there addressed the Elephant-King: 'Hope all goes well with you, Your Majesty!' and the Elephant-King asked, 'Who are you?'

Victory answered, 'I am an envoy.'

'An envoy in whose service?'

'I am in the service of the blessed Moon.'

'State your business,' said the Elephant-King.

'As you know, Your Majesty, an envoy on mission cannot be harmed, so I may speak freely. By command of the Moon, I am here to say that you have done violence to the Moon's subjects who lived beside the Lake of the Moon, his lake. You may not know your own strength or that of your followers, but you have trampled upon a whole colony of rabbits, despite the fact that everyone knows a rabbit lives with Lord Moon. Do not go to the Lake again or my Lord Moon's light will be withheld and you and your companions will perish.'

On hearing Victory's speech the Elephant-King realized his unwitting blunder and said, 'Please point me to where I must go to ask the blessed Moon's pardon.'

Victory then took the Elephant-King to a different part of the Lake and showed him the Moon reflected in its clear water. The Elephant-King tried to pay homage to the Lake by drinking gently from it. As he did so, his huge trunk disturbed the water and the reflection of the Moon became that of hundreds of Moons.

Victory cried out, 'Woe to you! You have enraged the blessed Moon. You should not have touched this lake's water!'

The Elephant-King pleaded, 'Please, Sir, please ask for forgiveness on my behalf and I promise never to come near this lake again or let my followers do so.'

'That is why I think the birds should not choose the Owl as king,' said the Crow. 'The Owl would be a sly judge and you should expect betrayal rather than protection. Remember how the rabbit and the partridge died confiding in the Cat.'

'Tell us,' begged the birds, and the Crow told them this story. ✍

Umpire Cat and His Ruling

'At one time of my life,' began the Crow, 'I lived in a maple tree in a city park. Underneath the same tree, there also lived a partridge. We liked each other and spent a lot of time together. One day the Partridge went in search of food with his other friends and did not return. I was quite concerned and when a month had gone by and he did not come back, I was sure he had had some kind of mishap and died. I grieved for my friend.

'More time passed and a rabbit made his home in the hole right next to the Partridge's nest. I didn't object. But soon thereafter the Partridge showed up again. He seemed very well fed and in good spirits and glad to be back home. When he saw the Rabbit, he scolded him for occupying his home.

'"Please leave as soon as possible," he said to the Rabbit who replied, "You are wrong. You can call a place yours only while you live in it."

'"OK, let us ask our neighbours," said the Partridge. "I will go by their opinion."

'But the Rabbit argued, "Even if your neighbours agree that you lived here for ten years, the place does not become yours, for that is the rule only among humans. For birds and beasts, presence is ownership. The place was unoccupied when I moved in, so now it is mine."

'"Clearly, we must go find someone else to take a fair view of this and decide," said the Partridge. So they took off to find a suitable umpire. Soon they ran into a cat who was a confidence trickster. It was only a matter of time before the Cat had both adversaries drawn into believing that he would be an impartial arbitrator. Still, the Partridge did not want to get too close to a natural enemy.

'To make a long story short, the rogue Cat won their confidence completely and they got too close to him. He wounded them both with one vicious swipe and quickly caught one in his teeth and the other in his claws. He killed and ate them both.'

'If you,' continued the Crow, 'make the Owl a second King, just think: he cannot see in the daytime, so what kind of judge will he be?'

All the birds flew off to their homes and only the Owl sat on his throne awaiting a coronation for he was blind by day. He called out, 'What is this delay? Where is everybody?'

Only a nearby owl heard him and replied, 'The Crow managed to find a way to stop the ceremony. All the birds have gone home. Only that Crow is still here.'

The Owl was deeply hurt and disappointed. He said to the Crow, 'I won't forget how you have wronged me. A cruel and ugly speech wounds so deeply that it never heals.' Then he went home.

'Oh dear,' the Crow thought. 'I have made an enemy needlessly. I should have considered the consequences before I voiced my opinion.'

*

'All right,' said King Spirit, 'having inherited this feud among crows and owls, what can we do now?'

Live-Strong said, 'I will have to deceive the enemy to conquer him just like the conman who robbed the Brahmin of his goat.'

'How so?' asked King Spirit, and Live-Strong told this story.

How the Brahmin Lost His Goat

There was once a pious Brahmin who was the keeper of the fire and had the job of making periodic animal sacrifices to it. In the middle of the winter with the new moon due, the Brahmin went to a neighbouring village to beg for an animal to sacrifice. A rich farmer gave him a well-fed goat that he tied up and swung on to his shoulder to take home.

On the way back, he ran into three cold and hungry wastrels who immediately saw their opportunity and plotted to get the goat from the Brahmin.

They first passed him by, but later the second one, having changed his appearance, came up and said, 'Holy Sir, why are you carrying a dog on your shoulder? You know a dog is an unclean animal and pollutes you.'

The Brahmin was truly offended and replied, 'Are you blind? You think my goat is a dog?'

'OK,' said the rogue, 'no need to get angry,' and went on his way.

Further along the road, the other two rogues disguised themselves and walked up to the Brahmin and said, 'Dear Sir, even if the dead calf was your pet, you should not carry it on your shoulder. It defiles you.'

The Brahmin got more irritated and said, 'Are you blind? You call my goat a calf?'

'OK, OK, no need to get angry,' said the two rogues 'Do whatever you want.' Saying this, they went away.

When the Brahmin was close to his home village, the three rogues, disguised, appeared yet again and said, 'Sir, carrying a donkey on your shoulder is most improper. You must drop it and go bathe and cleanse yourself at once.'

Very confused by then, the poor Brahmin, thinking that he was carrying some kind of demon that kept changing its shape, dropped the goat and ran home in a hurry. Of course, the three scoundrels made a feast of the goat.

Having finished the story, Live-Strong continued, 'Every man can be cheated by clever rogues. Also, it is better to cleverly avoid a quarrel with a crowd than pick a fight, for even if each member in it may be weak, an angry crowd is fearsome. Remember the ants that ate the giant snake?'

'How was that?' asked King Spirit, and Live-Strong told this story. ✍

How the Angry Ants Ate the Giant Snake

A giant black snake lived in a huge anthill. The ants were used to him coming and going via a large tunnel. One day he tried to crawl along a much narrower hole and got injured, for he was too big and because fate had willed it. The ants quickly smelled the odour of fresh blood and crawled all over the snake, which made him frantic. By thrashing around he crushed and killed lots and lots of ants. They became very, very angry and gathered in a huge crowd. By acting together, they stung the snake endlessly, all over until they killed him – and ate him up.

After finishing the story, Live-Strong continued, 'King Spirit, I have something to tell you, which you must consider very carefully. We must use deceit as a means to vanquish the Owl-King. Conciliation, intrigue, bribery and fighting will not work. You must pretend to completely turn against me, rail loudly about my faults and the bad advice I have given you, hit me and smear me with blood, and then leave me as if for dead at the base of our banyan tree. Then take your entire retinue of crows with you and fly off to Buffalo Mountain. You should stay there until I can win the trust of our enemy, find out the location of their fortress and destroy it. You must not feel any pity for me or try to stop me. For *while kings need to treat their servants well, even pamper them, when it comes to war, they must let them live or die in battle.*'

King Spirit did exactly what Live-Strong said. By this time it was getting dark and the owls were out and about. A scout owl had come near the banyan tree, saw how badly hurt Live-Strong was, and quickly flew back to the Owl-King with the news.

Seeing an opportunity, the Owl-King got his retinue together and organized a massive crow-hunt. With a harsh battle cry they flew to attack the crows in the banyan tree but found it completely empty of crows.

'Better search for the crows' line of retreat and kill them before they reach safety,' the Owl-King ordered.

Live-Strong heard the Owl-King and realized that it was time to draw their attention, for if they left, he would not be able to put his plan into action. So he squeaked feebly but loudly enough to alert the owls to his position. They quickly found him and took him to their king.

Live-Strong was able to explain: 'I was punished severely by my master because I advised that the crows not pick a fight with as strong an enemy as you are. Please help me and I will lead you to the crows' retreat.'

The Owl-King consulted his counsellors as to what they should do. The first, an advisor named Red-Eye, said immediately, 'Kill the crow. It is best to kill an enemy before he can recover and gain strength. A lost chance brings a curse.'

'How come?' asked the Owl-King, and Red-Eye told this story.

Snake Who Paid in Gold

Once there was a Brahmin who worked very hard and put in long hours. But his land remained quite barren. Towards the end of one summer, when he had been dozing under a tree, he saw a fearsome snake with his hood fanned out, looking directly at him from a nearby anthill.

Although he was scared, the Brahmin thought that perhaps the Snake was the guardian of his field and he had never paid him any honour. Perhaps that was why nothing grew on the field. So he got a saucer of milk from his home and presented it to the Snake, saying, 'Guardian of my field, I am sorry I did not know. I have paid you no respect. Please accept my offering and show your grace to me.' The Brahmin then went home.

The next day he found a gold coin where he had left the saucer of milk. He was very happy and from then on he left milk for the Snake every day and every morning the Snake left him a gold coin. After a few weeks had passed, the Brahmin had to go to a neighbouring village to buy seeds and told his son to take the saucer of milk to the Snake. The son did as asked.

The following morning, however, when he saw the gold coin, the greedy boy decided to kill the Snake and take the Snake's entire hoard of gold, which he was sure would be nearby. The Snake did not die when the boy tried to kill him and instead attacked the boy and bit him on the neck, killing him.

When the Brahmin returned and found out what had happened, he could only say, 'One should always be generous to all living creatures or your own life will slip away. Remember the swans and their Lotus Lake nest?'

'What happened there?' asked the Brahmin's grieving family, and the Brahmin told this story of the unfriendly swans.

Unfriendly Swans of Lotus Lake

Once there was a King named White Lotus who owned a beautiful lake named Lotus Lake after him. Many rare golden swans had made their home in the lake and people left them alone at the King's command because each swan paid him in a gold tail-feather every six months.

As time went by, a gorgeous, glittering, large gold bird arrived at the lake. The Golden Swans immediately challenged him.

'You cannot live among us on this lake for we rent all of it from the King by paying a gold tail-feather every six months.'

The Gold Bird said, 'You are very rude and unfriendly. I will not be any trouble to you.'

But the Golden Swans were adamant, so the Gold Bird offered to go talk to the King himself.

'What can the King do?' the Golden Swans said. 'We will not allow you to stay here.'

'You really are very impolite,' said the Gold Bird. 'I will tell the King this myself.'

When the King heard about the behaviour of the Golden Swans, he ordered his servants to kill all of them and have a great feast. One wise Golden Swan who saw the King's guard arriving told the rest of the flock that they would be destroyed unless they immediately fled, which they hurriedly did.

*

Next morning the Brahmin again took the saucer of milk to the Snake in his field and tried to win back his trust. 'My son met a death that he deserved,' said the Brahmin.

The Snake replied, '*You cannot break a heart and then hope to repair it, because the ache lives on forever.*'

The Owl-King turned next to another counsellor named Fierce-Eye and asked, 'What is your opinion?'

'Please don't listen to heartless advice,' answered Fierce-Eye. '*One does not kill a supplicant.* The Dove paid due respect to his mortal enemy who came as a supplicant to his door and died for it.'

'How was that?' asked the Owl-King, and Fierce-Eye told this story.

Doves' Sacrifice

There was once a cruel and vicious bird-hunter, a fowler, in a forest where all the birds lived in constant fear of losing their lives. The Fowler roamed the woods daily with his snare, net, cage and cudgel, always looking to catch and kill.

One afternoon in high summer, he was caught in a violent storm that completely drenched him and he sought shelter under a tree. He prayed for good fortune for he was cold and hungry.

In the same tree lived a pair of turtle doves who loved each other truly and faithfully. Before the storm, the Dove Wife had been caught by the Fowler and lay tied up in his net. The Dove Husband was miserable for his wife and bemoaning his bad fortune. 'A house is not a home when the mistress is missing,' he said. 'My wife is my true love.'

The ensnared Dove Wife heard her husband and called out, 'You are my loving husband and my very life. Listen to my difficult advice, please. Our enemy, the Fowler, lies in need of food and shelter at the bottom of our tree. Do not let your hate get the better of you. I was caught as a punishment for my sins, but you must help him.'

The poor broken-hearted Dove Husband went and found an ember from another's fire and started a bonfire for the Fowler so he would stop shivering. But he had no food to give. In his despair and love for his wife, he gave all he had left to the Fowler: he sacrificed his own body for his guest's hunger.

When the Fowler witnessed this sacrifice, he was so ashamed of the life he had led that he vowed to seek virtue no matter the cost. He freed the Dove Wife. But when she realized her husband was gone, she grieved for him.

'I cannot live without my love, my sweet husband,' she said and walked straight into the fire. As she did so, she saw a blinding light and her husband awaiting her with his arms wide open. She went right into them and the two flew straight to heaven for a long, loving and blissful life together.

The Fowler, faced with the self-sacrifice of the turtle doves, could not stop himself. He too walked into the burning bush, cleansed away his sins and also reached heaven.

Having heard the tale, the Owl-King turned to his trustworthy counsellor and asked, 'Flame-Eye, what should I do?' and the counsellor recounted the following story. 🖋

Old Man Who Had a Young Wife

A rich old merchant lost his wife and decided to marry a young wife. Of course, no young girl wants to wed a very old man, so he had to pay a heavy price to a penniless shopkeeper to marry his young daughter.

As one would expect, few people love those who are old. Often even a son pays little honour to a doddering old father. Anyway, the young wife was shy and even though she missed talking to her family, she didn't want to speak with the old man or even look at him. She always turned her face away from her husband

and said little to him. But one night she suddenly turned towards him and hugged him tight.

'Oh ho! What's happening here!' thought the old man. 'She never even looks at me otherwise, but is now embracing me.' So he looked around very carefully and saw a thief cowering in a corner of the bedroom.

Then, the old man said to the thief, 'Thank you. You are my benefactor. Take whatever you like.'

The thief replied, 'Actually, there is little here I want to steal. But if I want something I will return, and I *will* return if your wife will no longer cling to you!'

'Therefore', Flame-Eye continued, 'you shouldn't kill the crow. A thief can become a benefactor and a supplicant an ally. Because the crow was badly treated he will help us all the more, and once we discover the weak points of our enemy, we will destroy him. Remember, if there be discord in the enemy's ranks, the thief loses his cows, and the ghost loses his meals.'

'How was that?' asked the Owl-King, and the counsellor told this story.

Brahmin, Thief and Demon Ghost

There was a very poor Brahmin who lived on the alms that people gave him. It was a hard life. He looked terrible – dishevelled and unhealthy – for he had to live on the street all year – in the heat, cold and rain. One day a rich farmer took pity on him and gave him two calves. The Brahmin managed to raise them well and they became quite plump, even though he begged others for his own food. The two cows became his lifeline.

One day, a thief saw the two cows and at once made plans to steal them from the Brahmin. So that night, the Thief got some thick rope and started walking to where the Brahmin lived with the cows.

On his way, he met a horrible looking creature with a deformed body and fearsome eyes. He looked like he had escaped from purgatory.

The Thief was scared and asked, 'Who are you?' and the other replied, 'I am a Demon Ghost and I try to get at the truth. Now it is your turn to introduce yourself.'

The Thief answered truthfully. 'I am a cruel thief. I am on my way to steal two cows from a poor Brahmin.'

The Demon Ghost laughed and said, 'I will join you. I eat every three days and it is eating day today. I am hungry and will eat this Brahmin. Let us go.' So together they walked to the Brahmin's hut and waited until he was sound asleep.

Then the Demon Ghost made the first move towards the Brahmin, but the Thief stopped him. 'Hey! Wait a minute. This is not right. You cannot attack the Brahmin until I have taken the cows.'

But the Demon Ghost said, 'The noise you will make tying up the cows and getting them out will wake the Brahmin and he will escape.'

The Thief replied, 'If something happens when you try to eat the poor Brahmin, I will not be able to steal the cows.' So the two enemies of the Brahmin began to argue.

The Brahmin heard them and watched with half-closed eyes. Seeing the Demon Ghost, he first said a prayer to his favourite God for protection. And as the Demon Ghost began to disappear, the Brahmin picked up a cudgel and saved his two cows from the Thief.

'Besides,' continued the counsellor to the Owl-King, 'it is written in the scriptures that it is wrong to kill a supplicant. Do not kill the Crow.'

The Owl-King turned to yet another counsellor, 'What do you say?' The counsellor, named Wall-Eared, said, 'You should certainly not kill the Crow. If you spare his life, you may well grow to like him and become friends. But remember also that *it is better to keep secrets in the give and take of mutual defence*, or you may perish like the snake in the belly and the snake in the anthill.'

'Please explain.' said the Owl-King, and the counsellor told this story.

Snake in the Prince's Belly

In a city-state called Janga lived a King named Divine. He had a son who was wasting away because he had a parasitic snake who lived in his belly. The Prince was very depressed because he could not live a normal life and that made his parents very sad. So he left and went to another city in another state and there he lived on alms and spent most of his time in a big temple.

The King of that city, named Offering, had two daughters. One bowed daily to her father saying, 'Victory to you, O King' while the other greeted him with, 'Just Deserts, Dear King'. The King was at first irritated by the second daughter and eventually became very angry with her for persisting with her greeting. He ordered his ministers to give her away in marriage to a foreigner so that *she* would get her 'just deserts'. And so they wedded her off to the Prince who was an outsider and lived a simple life in the temple.

The young bride happily accepted the Prince as her husband and together they left to go to another place far away from her family. There they found a house by the edge of a pond. The Prince stayed in the yard while the Princess went grocery shopping with their servant. When she came home she found the Prince asleep with his head resting on an anthill. From his mouth emerged the head of a hooded snake who was looking directly at another snake emerging from the anthill. Both snakes were hissing at each other.

The anthill-snake said, 'You villain! How can you torment this poor Prince by living in his belly?' And the other snake said, 'How come you hoard two pots of gold in your anthill?' They kept arguing for a while. The anthill-snake said, 'The Prince only has to drink black mustard oil to get rid of you!' and the belly-snake replied, 'Boiling water poured in the anthill would destroy *you*!'

As it happened, the Princess had overheard the snakes. She proceeded to use the methods the snakes had themselves mentioned to destroy them both. She made her husband well, dug up the two pots of gold, and returned home to live happily ever after. She got her 'just deserts'!

The Owl-King was finally convinced to spare the life of the Crow Live-Strong. But the counsellor Red-Eye was displeased and said to the other counsellors, 'Our master is ruined by your bad advice and has forgiven a clear offence. Remember how the carpenter was duped by his faithless wife and her wicked lover?'

'How was that?' asked the counsellors and Red-Eye told this story.

Carpenter, Duped by his Wife

There was a Carpenter married to an unfaithful wife. The whole village knew that she was a bad woman and rumours had reached the Carpenter. So one day, he started off to test her fidelity. He told her that he was going to a neighbouring village on a two-day job and would she please pack him enough food to take with him, which she did very willingly.

The minute the Carpenter left, his wife sent a message to her lover that she was free and asked him to come over that night. Meanwhile, the Carpenter returned home and sneaked into the bedroom and hid under the bed.

That night the wife's lover went to bed first. So the Carpenter knew his wife was unfaithful. But still he waited and remained hidden to see what would happen.

As the wife was about to get into bed, she accidentally kicked something under the bed. She immediately grasped the true situation. Her husband had set a trap and she had walked into it! But she was a clever cheat. So she stood by the bed and asked her lover to listen. 'I am a good woman and love my husband,' she said. 'I asked you to come here because this morning the fortune-teller told me that my husband's life is in danger and that the only way to avert widowhood is for me to disgrace myself by sleeping with a man not my husband.'

The lover understood what the wife was trying to hint at and he played along and had fun. The stupid, gullible, good Carpenter swallowed the deception hook, line and sinker, and ran all over the village singing their praises. Everyone, of course, laughed behind his back.

'That's why I say,' continued Red-Eye, 'shrewd men try to unmask a foe who seems a friend.' But the other counsellors disregarded his wisdom and picked up Live-Strong to take him to the Owl-King's fortress.

Live-Strong then asked the Owl-King, 'Why are you so kind to me, O King? I have done nothing yet to deserve it. Please place me in your debt forever by seating me near a fire.'

Red-Eye suspected something was up and asked, 'Why do you wish to be close to a fire?'

Live-Strong replied, 'I was beaten nearly to death for your sake. Now all I want is to cleanse myself in the fire and be reborn as an owl to take revenge on the crows.'

Red-Eye, a master of diplomacy, said, 'Even if born as an owl, you would find the crows sympathetic and a kindred kind, for no one forgets one's origins. Remember the mouse-maid? Even though the mouse-turned-girl had suitors like the Sun, Cloud, Wind and Mountain, she chose a mouse and went back to her own natural species.'

'Please explain,' said Live-Strong, and Red-Eye told this story.

Once a Mouse, Always a Mouse

There was once a holy man who lived by the shores of a mighty river that cascaded down high mountains. The Holy Man had magical powers, but he lived simply with his wife within a community of like-minded pious people. The Wife had no children, which made her sad.

One day, as the Holy Man was bathing in the river, a tiny, beautiful baby mouse fell right into his hands from the claws of a hawk flying overhead. He wondered what he should do and then thought about his wife. He decided to change the baby mouse into a little baby girl and took her home. His Wife was delighted and raised her as her own daughter until she became of marriageable age.

Then, the wife said to her husband, 'It is time for our daughter to marry. Please find a suitable husband for her.' The Holy Man thought it important to give her in marriage to someone of her own station. 'Where wealth is comparable and the family status is the same, marriages work out well,' he thought, 'but it never works between rich and poor. Seven things are needed for a successful marriage: money, good looks, learning, good family,

youth, position and virtue. So, if she agrees, I will give her to the Sun who lights up the whole world.'

'No, Father,' said the Girl. 'He is burning hot. Please find another groom.'

So the Holy Man asked the Sun, 'Is there anyone superior to you?'

'Yes,' said the Sun, 'the Cloud. When he comes in front of me, I disappear.'

'No, Father,' said the Girl, 'the Cloud is too gloomy and cold. Please find me another groom.'

So the Holy Man asked the Cloud, 'Is there anyone superior to you?'

'Yes,' said the Cloud, 'the Wind. He can blow me away.'

'No, Father,' said the Girl, 'the Wind is too restless and flighty. Please find another.'

So the Holy Man asked the Wind, 'Is there anyone superior to you?'

'Yes,' said the Wind, 'the Mountain. No one can move him.'

'No, Father,' said the Girl, 'the Mountain is stubborn and rocky. Please find another groom.'

So the Holy Man asked the Mountain, 'Is there anyone superior to you?'

'Yes,' said the Mountain, 'the Mouse. He can make holes in my entire body.'

'Yes, please,' said the Girl. 'I would be happy to wed a mouse.' So the Holy Man turned her back into a mouse and she lived happily ever after with her mouse husband.

However, no one paid attention to Red Eye's story. The Owls took the Crow to their fortress and Live-Strong had a good laugh. He thought, 'They could have and should have killed me without having to pay any price.'

When they reached the fortress, the Owl-King told his servants, 'Give the Crow any room he likes. He is our well-wisher.'

Live-Strong figured out that in order to destroy the fortress he would need to stay near the entrance. So he said to the Owl-King, 'O King, I wish you well, but I also know my place. I will not stay in the heart of the fortress but near the entrance and pay my daily homage from there.'

The Owl-King agreed and ordered the servants to take good care of the Crow.

However, Red-Eye was disturbed by how Live-Strong was being pampered and told the Owl-King and his counsellors, 'You are all being taken in. Remember the song, "I played the fool first, followed by he who tethered me, then king and counsellor; We were all fools together."'

'How so?' asked a counsellor, and Red-Eye told this story.

Bird with Gold Droppings

On the side of a very high mountain, there was a very big tree in which lived a bird with gold droppings.

One day a hunter who was also an accomplished fowler was passing by when the bird's dropping fell on the ground directly in front of him. It had turned golden the moment it had come out of the Bird.

The Hunter was amazed. He had never seen such a thing in his entire life! So he set a snare and the foolish Bird got caught immediately. Then the Hunter took the Bird out of the snare, put him in a cage, and took him home.

However, the Hunter was very worried because it seemed to him the Bird could be an ill-omen. If other people saw the Bird's peculiar droppings of gold, they would be sure to report him to the King and his very life could be in danger. So he himself decided to take the Bird to the King.

When the King saw the Bird and heard the Hunter's story, he was pleased. He told his attendants to care for the Bird, and give him plenty to eat and drink.

'Why do you keep the Bird, O King?' asked a counsellor. 'He was hatched from an ordinary egg. You have only the Hunter's word of the gold droppings. You have no other proof. Have you ever known there to be gold in a bird's dropping? Set the Bird free.' The King was gullible and took his counsellor's advice and set the Bird free.

At this point the Bird flew up to a high parapet in the palace, made a dropping of gold and flew away singing, 'First me, then Hunter, then King, then Counsellor; all fools together.'

But no one paid any attention to Red-Eye's story and advice. They continued to pamper Live-Strong, who was now completely recovered from his beating by the Crow King Spirit.

Finally, Red-Eye gathered his personal staff in private and said, 'The end is near. The King and the fortress will soon be in ruins. I have given my best advice, but the Owl-King will not listen. It is now time for us to seek another fortress. Planning ahead is so much better than getting caught unawares. Remember the cave that talked?'

'How was that?' asked his staff, and Red-Eye told this story.

Talking Cave

There was a deep cave in a mountainside where a jackal named Planner lived. He was a very cautious jackal and always checked to see whether the cave was safe to enter.

One day, as the sun was about to set, a lion named Crusher was passing by the same cave. He thought to himself that some wild animal was bound to come into the cave for shelter at night, so he hid inside and waited.

When the Jackal returned, he called out, 'O Cave, O Cave, How goes it?'

He waited awhile and then called out again: 'O Cave, why won't you speak to me? We had a deal that when I come to you and call out, you would answer me promptly.'

Again he waited for some time and said, 'OK, I will go to the other cave, which will probably be more polite than you.'

Upon hearing the Jackal, the Lion thought to himself that the Cave was not answering because he sensed that the Lion was there and was afraid to do so. 'I will answer the Jackal's greeting myself,' the Lion thought, 'and when he enters, I'll make a meal of him.'

So the Lion roared a greeting that echoed deeply in the cave and terrified all the creatures who heard it. The Jackal, of course, fled, thinking it is always wise to know what to fear, and plan ahead.

'So,' said Red-Eye to his staff, 'come with me,' and they all left in search of a safe home.

Live-Strong was delighted to see them go. He knew Red-Eye was learned and far-sighted, and could have posed a problem because a shrewd counsellor can discover enemies disguised as friends. Meanwhile, as each day passed, Live-Strong collected an ember from the forest fires and hid it in his own nest.

The Owls had no idea about what he was up to. He just seemed to be building a nest, but Live-Strong had collected quite a woodpile at the fortress gate. Every morning, when the Owls turned blind, he went out and reported to his own king about what he was doing.

One day, he was ready and said to King Spirit, 'I have made the enemy's cave ready for burning. Please come quickly with all your retinue and with each crow bringing a lit stick to throw on my nest at the entrance to the Owls' fortress. Then all your enemies will burn to death. Please be quick, there is no time to lose.'

King Spirit followed Live-Strong's advice to the letter

and the Crows exterminated the Owls, and returned safely to their home in the banyan tree.

Once enthroned comfortably, King Spirit asked Live-Strong to recount his time in the enemy camp.

'Most of the owls were fools,' replied Live-Strong, 'but one, Red-Eye, had great intelligence, learning and insight, and correctly gauged my purpose and strategy. The other counsellors were dimwits even as they pretended to give sage advice to the Owl-King. And the Owl-King was not at all aware that *a prudent ruler guards himself by being well-advised. The steady forfeit glory, the restless forfeit friends, the bankrupt forfeit family, bankers forfeit wealth, the passionate forfeit learning, the careless forfeit followers, and kings forfeit kingly power – all because of taking bad advice.* My time in the enemy camp was a test of endurance, but in the end it paid off. Remember how the great black snake killed all the frogs?'

'How was that?' asked King Spirit, and Live-Strong told this story. ✒

Frogs That Rode Snake-back

Once, an old black snake called Fang was basking in the sun on a rock and taking stock of his life. He was now pretty old and was having trouble catching prey. So he decided on a plan and went to a nearby pond where there were many frogs. He lay about on the edge of the water, looking obviously very depressed.

Seeing him doing nothing, a curious frog approached and asked him, 'How come you are not hunting for food?'

'I am in real trouble,' replied Fang. 'Earlier this evening, I was going to creep up on a frog, but he saw me in time and hopped into the middle of a group of holy men and their families. I tried to follow the frog but mistakenly bit a Brahmin boy's toe, which looked like a frog. The boy died. The father Brahmin was so angry that he put a curse on me. "You killed an innocent boy who did you no harm," he cried. "You will be damned from now on and will be completely dependent on frogs. You will be a vehicle for the frogs and they will ride on your back. You will live only on whatever the frogs allow you to eat."

'So you see,' said Fang, 'I am entirely at your mercy.'

The curious frog, satisfied that he had heard the truth, repeated the amazing story to all other frogs in the pond. They were delighted to hear that the black snake they dreaded would now be their vehicle. So they all rode the snake that day.

The next day Fang moved very slowly. So much so that the Frog-King asked the Snake, 'Why are you not carrying me as well as you did yesterday?

Fang replied, 'Because I am starving. You have not fed me anything at all.' So the Frog-King allowed Fang to eat some small, low-born frogs. But Fang did not stop there. He kept eating frogs until he grew really strong. He was very pleased with his trickery and wondered how long the frogs would last.

The very next day another black snake

came by and saw Fang giving rides to frogs. Irritated, he asked Fang, 'Why are you carrying our natural food on your back?'

Fang answered, 'I am simply marking time like the butter-blind Brahmin!'

'How so?' asked the Snake, and Fang told this story.

Brahmin's Revenge

There was a Brahmin, named Believer, whose wife was unfaithful. She was always running after other men and often baked them cakes with lots of sugar and butter, thereby shortchanging her husband.

One day, Believer saw her and asked, 'What are you making? And where do you take all the cakes you bake? Tell me the truth.'

But the quick, clever cheat was ready with a lie: 'There is a shrine of the blessed Goddess nearby where I participate in a fasting ceremony and take delicious cakes as an offering.' Then she left for the shrine but went first to the river for a cleansing bath.

The Brahmin, who had deliberately taken a different road, arrived at the shrine before his wife and proceeded to hide behind the statue of the Goddess. The Wife appeared shortly thereafter having completed her obligatory rituals. She bowed to the Goddess and prayed, 'Please help me. How may I make my husband blind?'

The Brahmin was stunned to hear his wife's prayer, but with great presence of mind answered in a disguised voice, 'Feed him mostly butter and butter-cakes, and he will eventually go blind.'

Sure enough the Wife began feeding her husband butter and butter-cakes and after a few days Believer said to his Wife, 'I don't see too well. I may be going blind,' hearing which the Wife thanked the Goddess in her heart.

Meanwhile, the Wife's lover began visiting her at her home daily because he too thought the husband had gone blind and so he had nothing to fear. However, after a fortnight or so, the Brahmin was ready for his revenge. When the lover came, he picked up a cudgel and clubbed him to death. Then he cut off his Wife's nose so the whole village would know of her infidelity.

*

When Fang finished telling the story, the other snake took off. Needless to say, when Fang had bided his time sufficiently, he ate up all the frogs in the pond.

After the story, King Spirit said, 'There is greatness in seeing an undertaking through.'

And Live-Strong replied, '*Valour is not sufficient for victory. Wit and wisdom can destroy fame, family and royal possessions.*'

The King added '*Kingship only survives with prudence, courage and strength for self-sacrifice. One must be ever vigilant of a friend and never trust a foe.*'

Monkey and Crocodile

About this Book

Book Four here titled 'Monkey and Crocodile' deals with how to protect and preserve any gains you have made in life, no matter in what area. Most of the loss-of-gain stories are told by the Monkey who fooled the Crocodile into freeing him from sure death by telling a clever story. Many of the Monkey's stories are about the use of deceit to improve one's position, or to protect oneself. And the losers are foolish enough to be tricked out of their gains by a sweet-talking enemy. They are gullible and deserve what they get. Husbands will, apparently, do anything for their wives and sometimes pay a heavy price. And wives – like the Crocodile's wife in the *frame* story – are typically shown as demanding and unreasonable. Deceit, when exposed, can lead to the deceiver's undoing. One should be humble before the noble, use trickery when one cannot win advantage by strength, offer a lure when necessary, pick a fight only with equals and give good advice only to those best able to use it.

The frame story then is about the Monkey and the Crocodile. They discuss the situation they are in and justify their viewpoints through tales that form most of the book's *nesting* stories. These, mostly single *stand-alone* stories, are separated in this presentation from the main one in a simple way: the frame story of the two friends who with the text enclosed become adversaries is located on the coloured pages and can be read without interruption, while the white pages tell the stand-alone and nesting stories. This allows readers to choose how they want to read the book – just the frame story or just selected nesting stories, or both sequentially to experience the original design of the book. ✍

Monkey and Crocodile

The fourth set of teaching tales Sharma told was:
Monkey and Crocodile.

Sharma began:

'Only a fool parts with gains
When sweet-talked out of them
And then must pay the price
The Monkey exacted from
The Crocodile.'

'How come?' asked the three Princes, and Sharma
told this story.

Monkey and Crocodile

There was a great big rose-apple tree that grew close to the bank of an enormous river. It bore delicious fruit that ripened every day and was enjoyed immensely by a red-faced monkey named Ruddy.

One day a crocodile named Oily crawled out of the river on to the bank and burrowed into the soft sand. Ruddy saw him and welcomed his guest. 'No one is more important than a guest to me, no matter how unexpected,' he said. 'Please accept these scrumptious rose-apples that I throw down to you as my offering.'

Oily enjoyed them very much, spent time in easy conversation with Ruddy and took some rose-apples home to his wife.

'Where did you find these?' she asked. 'They are like ambrosia.'

'I have made a new friend, Ruddy, and he gets them from the tree and gives them to me,' replied Oily.

Then the wife reasoned that if the monkey ate such heavenly fruit every day, he must have a heart with extraordinary powers. So she said to Oily, 'If you value me at all, please bring me the monkey's heart so that after I eat it, I will never grow old or sick but will be your loving wife forever.'

Oily objected strongly. 'Ruddy is like a brother to me now. Remember, brothers by friendship are even more precious than brothers by birth. He gives me this wonderful fruit every day. I cannot kill him!'

But the wife was adamant. 'You have never said no to me before. You must love this she-monkey more than you love me and if this is a male monkey, why do you love him? Monkeys and crocodiles are natural enemies. Bring me his heart or I will die of starvation for I will eat nothing else.' Completely dejected, Oily returned to the rose-apple tree, thinking, 'How can I possibly kill my friend?'

Ruddy had missed his friend and upon seeing him return, said cheerfully, 'What shall we discuss today as we eat the rose-apples?'

'My wife is very upset that I have not invited you home,' replied Oily. 'She has prepared a great welcome for you. So come with me.'

Ruddy was delighted and replied, 'I hold the six aspects of friendship very dear: to receive, to give, to listen, to talk, to dine and to entertain. But we monkeys live in trees and you live in water. How can I come to your house? Please bring your wife here.'

'Our house is on a sandbank,' said Oily, 'and you will

be quite comfortable there. No need to worry. Just climb on my back and I will take you there.'

So Ruddy climbed upon the crocodile's back, but when Oily took off at considerable speed, Ruddy was frightened and asked Oily to slow down. But Oily knew that Ruddy was out of his depth in the fast-moving water and now completely in his power. He could not stop himself from bragging, 'My wife wants to eat your heart. Better say your last prayers!'

Ruddy was, however, very quick-witted and said immediately, 'Why didn't you tell me on the shore? I have a second heart that I keep in my hole in the rose-apple tree. That one is my sweet heart. The heart I carry around is very ordinary and will not do your wife any good.'

Oily was delighted. Now he could give his wife the monkey's sweet heart and still have a friend. So he turned back to the shore and helped Ruddy climb high up the rose-apple tree.

Ruddy, meanwhile, was thinking, '*One should never be too trusting*. I have escaped death and thus am reborn today.'

After waiting a while, Oily shouted up to Ruddy, 'Give me the heart then, so I can make my wife happy, and be back at the regular time and talk about interesting things.'

'You are not only a traitor but a fool!' said Ruddy. 'How can anyone have two hearts? Don't ever come back here. Remember the proverb: *If you trust a faithless friend twice, death is certain.*'

Oily tried once more to win Ruddy back. 'I was just trying to test you,' he said. 'It was all a joke. Just come with me and be our guest.'

'Go away!' said Ruddy. 'Remember the story of Mr Handsome and the Frog-King.'

'Tell me, tell me,' said the Crocodile and the Monkey told this story.

Vindictive Frog-King

There was a Frog-King who lived in a well with a water wheel. He was sick of having relatives beg him for favours and decided to leave the well. He hopped carefully from bucket to bucket of the water-wheel and succeeded in getting out of the deep well.

Once out, however, the Frog-King began to brood on how to get even with his relatives. Just then he noticed a sleek but deadly black snake that people had nicknamed Mr Handsome.

'I know,' he said to himself, 'I will lead this snake into my well and he will kill all those awful relatives who made my life so miserable. They do say the wise use one foe to destroy another.' So the Frog-King approached Mr Handsome and made his proposition to him.

Mr Handsome was doubtful. He and the Frog-King were natural enemies, but the Frog-King convinced him that the deal could only benefit Mr Handsome because the Frog-King promised to give the serpent a frog a day. Mr Handsome agreed and made his way down to the

bottom of the well with the help of the Frog-King. But, of course, he did not stop with only the frogs that the Frog-King wanted killed as payback.

One day Mr Handsome ate the Frog-King's own son. The Queen was horrified and blamed the Frog-King. 'No point in howling now!' she said. 'Find a way for us to escape or think of a way to kill the serpent.'

Eventually, only the Frog-King was left alive, so Mr Handsome said to him, 'Friend, all the frogs are gone and I am hungry. Get me some food.'

'No problem,' said the Frog-King. 'If you allow me, I shall go to another well and get all the frogs living there to come over to this well.' Mr Handsome was delighted. 'You have been a brother to me. May you succeed in your scheme.' The Frog-King finally escaped from the well and went as far away as he could.

After a very long time, Mr Handsome saw a lizard in the well and asked her for a favour. 'Please, pretty please, go look for the Frog-King and tell him I miss him and that even if he comes alone I promise not to hurt him.'

The lizard delivered the message to the Frog-King who said, 'Go, fair lady, and tell Mr Handsome – the Frog-King will never return to that well.'

'And that is why,' said Ruddy, 'I will never enter your home.'

'Please, please,' said Oily, 'if you don't come, I will sit here and starve to death.'

'You idiot!' said Ruddy. 'Am I like Long Ears that I will go to a place of clear and certain death?'

'What happened to Long Ears?' asked Oily, and Ruddy told this story.

Long Ears and Muddy

A lion named Ferocious lived in a jungle with his loyal servant, a jackal named Muddy. One day Ferocious had a nasty fight with an elephant and was badly wounded. Since the lion could not go hunting and kill animals for food, poor Muddy also had to do without. When he could take it no more, he said to his master, 'O King, I can barely move from hunger, so how should I serve you?'

Ferocious replied, 'Bring me an animal that I can kill, even in my present state.'

So Muddy went hunting near a village and came across a donkey named Long Ears who was himself weak and thin and having trouble munching on tough grass.

Muddy went up to Long Ears and asked, 'How did you get so feeble?'

'I have a terrible master,' replied Long Ears. 'He overloads me and doesn't feed me enough. So I eat this tough grass, but it does not agree with me.'

Muddy offered, 'Come live with me. I know a spot with soft, green grass by the river.'

'But I cannot live in a forest – the wild animals will kill me,' said Long Ears. But Muddy was a clever jackal and succeeded in luring the poor donkey to the forest by promising him a beautiful wife.

Long Ears went into the lion's den, but Ferocious, in

his eagerness to kill, somehow overshot his spring and the donkey escaped.

Then Muddy asked Ferocious, 'What on earth happened?'

'I had no time to prepare my spring,' said Ferocious. 'You had better get me another animal.'

'You prepare a better spring for I will get Long Ears to come back,' said Muddy.

'How can you entice Long Ears back when he saw the danger first-hand?' asked Ferocious.

'Never mind,' said the Jackal and went after the donkey. 'Long Ears, you must return. The fearsome animal you saw was just your wife-to-be who was so excited to see you. You are shy, but you should not have run away.'

So the gullible Long Ears returned with Muddy to the lion's den a second time and was killed instantly by Ferocious. But before feasting on him, Ferocious decided to go bathe in the river and left Muddy in charge of the kill. When he returned, the jackal had already feasted on the heart and ears of the donkey.

Ferocious shouted angrily, 'You rogue, you have eaten the best parts and left the remains for your master!'

Muddy was ready with his response. 'I did no such thing, O King. The donkey had no heart or ears, otherwise he would not have forgotten his fear and returned to face certain death.'

Ferocious accepted the explanation and they dined on the rest of the poor dead donkey.

'I am *not* Long Ears,' continued Ruddy to Oily.

'You played a trick on me but then spoiled it by telling the truth, so you lost your gains just like the feisty Potter.'

'How was that?' asked the Crocodile, and the Monkey told this story. ✒

Feisty Potter

Once there was a potter named Honest, who had a terrible accident. He cut his forehead open very badly after falling over one of his broken pots with a jagged edge. The cut healed but Honest looked horribly ugly.

One year, when his business as a potter was failing and there was a famine, Honest decided to leave the area where he lived and become a guard elsewhere. In this new town, the King happened to see him, noticed his scar and concluded that Honest must be a war hero. Believing this, he showed the Potter great respect, showered him with honours and gifts until even his own sons became jealous – although they kept quiet.

A day came when the King was reviewing his best battalion of soldiers. Around him, elephants and horses were being readied for battle. The King saw the Potter among the spectators and asked him, 'Prince, who are you? Where is your family? In what war were you wounded?'

Honest readily explained how he had got his horrible scar. The King was so angry at his own mistake that he immediately ordered a flogging for Honest.

The Potter said to the King, 'Please, your Majesty, don't treat me like this but see how good I am in battle.'

The King answered, 'Be gone. You may be handsome, brave and bright, but in your family no elephants are slain.'

'How so?' asked Honest and the King told this story.

Jackal Raised by a Lioness

A Lion lived in a dense forest with his mate. Time passed and the Lioness gave birth to twin cubs. The parents were pleased and raised them together, the Lion providing the food and the Lioness the caring for the cubs.

One day the Lion searched far and wide but could find no food for his family. On the way back to his den he came upon a scrawny baby jackal. Full of pity, the Lion picked him up by the scruff of his neck and took him home for his wife to raise him. They both knew they could not eat him. They knew that the Gods frowned on anyone who strikes a holy man, a woman or a child, and the baby jackal was like a child. So the baby Jackal grew up in the Lion family thinking that the Lion cubs were his brothers and he began behaving like them.

When the cubs were half grown, a wild elephant came wandering. The two Lion cubs were eager to try their strength and wanted to kill the elephant. But the Jackal said, 'The elephant is an enemy of our race. Leave him alone,' and ran home as fast as he could.

Later, the Lion Cubs told their mother what happened. The Jackal felt humiliated. He was so angry that he wanted to kill his own brothers and said so to his mother. While she tried to calm him down, the Lioness realized it was time to give her adopted cub the truth.

'You are handsome, brave and bright, but in your birth family, my boy, no elephants were ever slain. You are a jackal raised by a lioness. It is time now to return to your own kind.'

The poor Jackal left immediately. 'That is why, you poor potter,' said the King, 'I suggest you leave right away before the other soldiers make fun of you and kill you.' The Potter fled.

'You really are a fool,' Ruddy continued chiding Oily. *'Never trust a woman. Remember the plight of the man who left his family and gave half his life to his wife who left him without a single thought.'*

"How so?' asked the Crocodile and the Monkey told this story. ✍

Ungrateful Wife

A long time ago there lived a Brahmin who loved his wife more than life itself. But she had a nasty temper and quarrelled every day with one or other members of the extended family with whom the couple lived after they were married.

The poor Brahmin found the situation intolerable and eventually left his family to go live elsewhere, far away.

On the way they had to pass through a great forest. The Wife said to her husband that she was very thirsty and could he please get her some water. When the Brahmin returned with some water, he found his Wife lying on the ground, dead. Stricken with overwhelming grief, he immediately started praying. He begged the Gods to give him back his Wife no matter what the cost.

'Even half your life?' was the answer from on high and he said 'Yes' quite happily. He was instructed to recite the required prayers and say 'I give life' three times. Lo and behold, his Wife got better and they continued their journey.

When they reached the outskirts of a town, the Brahmin asked his Wife to wait at the gates where there was a nice park while he went in search for food. When he was gone, the Wife met a handsome young cripple and fell in love at first sight. She cajoled him into sleeping with her and when the husband returned she asked him to help carry the cripple so they could all be together.

Thoroughly confused, the Brahmin objected saying, 'I can barely carry myself, how can I carry him?' The Wife, however, offered to carry the cripple in a basket on her head to which the bewildered husband agreed and they continued their journey to town.

When the Wife noticed a well near the path they were travelling, she signalled her lover to help push the Brahmin into the well, which they did! Having got rid of the husband, the Wife walked on towards the centre of the town with her lover still in the basket that she carried on her head. But she came up to a toll gate where the guards asked her to pay toll for whatever she had in the basket. When she wouldn't, they took the covered basket to the King and the Wife followed.

When she was in the presence of the King, she concocted a story: 'Your Majesty, the cripple is my husband. First my relatives married me to him, but then so mistreated him and me that I had to leave. My love and honour for my husband would not allow me to leave him behind. So I carry him in a basket on my head.' The King was so touched by the love story that he gave her and the cripple a couple of villages so they could live comfortably.

But the Brahmin was not dead. He managed to get out of the well and went after his Wife and lover. Their quarrel brought them before the King once again.

The Wife, of course, accused the husband of being one of the relatives who had mistreated her and the cripple. The Brahmin, however, kept his cool when the King was about to order his execution.

He said, 'Your Majesty, my wife, this woman, has something that belongs to me. For the sake of justice, would you please order her to return it so I can die happy?' The King granted his last request and the Brahmin asked his Wife to return the half of his life he had given her. Although she protested loudly that she had nothing of his, the Brahmin said his prayers and asked his Wife to repeat 'I give life' three times.

Since the Wife dared not refuse the King's order she did what the Brahmin asked and after she had spoken she fell down dead. The King was astonished and wanted to hear a full explanation that the Brahmin happily gave.

She was an ungrateful wife.

Having told the story, Ruddy went on, 'But there is another tale even more apt for highlighting the same moral: Men will do anything if asked by a wife – shaving their heads out of season, or saying anything, even neighing like a horse.'

'What are you talking about?' said the Crocodile. 'Tell me,' and the Monkey told this story. ✍

Two Henpecked Husbands

Once there was a King named Magnificent, renowned for his wealth and power. He had a minister named Meritorious, whom he trusted and who was extremely learned in all the arts and sciences. But each had a problem.

The Minister adored his wife but even he had a lover's quarrel one day, and his wife would no longer speak to him. He begged her forgiveness and promised he would do whatever she asked. His Wife eventually relented but on the condition that he would shave his head for her.

The King had also gotten into an argument with the Queen. Although it was a trivial matter, she had stopped speaking to him. He asked her pardon for his part in the argument and asked what he could do as penance. The Queen thought it over and said, 'If you pretend to be a horse, take a horse's bit in your mouth and neigh like a horse, all shall be forgiven.'

Having told the story, Ruddy continued to rebuke Oily. 'You are an idiot! You too are henpecked like the King and his Minister. You undertook to kill me because your wife demanded it. Remember parrots and mynah birds are caged because they mimic words. Even the well-disguised ass was killed because he opened his mouth.'

'How was that?' asked the Crocodile, and the Monkey told this story. ✍

Ass in the Tiger Skin

There was a laundryman named Clean White, who lived in a small town. He had a donkey who had grown thin and weak because the owner was unable to give him good feed.

One day, Clean White was wandering in a nearby forest when he saw a dead tiger. He immediately wondered how he could use the tiger skin. He thought up a plan to dress his donkey in the tiger skin and let him go out at night to graze in the neighbour's barley fields. He was sure that when the watchful farmers saw a tiger in their fields they would leave him alone. So Clean White took the dead tiger home and skinned it.

The laundryman's plan worked perfectly: The donkey could feed well every night, became quite fat and could work well for Clean White during the day. Time passed and one night when the ass in the tiger skin was eating in the barley fields, he heard the call of a she-donkey in the distance. So, of course, the donkey

brayed in answer. The farmers realized that the tiger they were avoiding was just a disguised donkey. They were very angry. They chased the donkey, caught it and killed it.

Now, while the Monkey Ruddy was telling the Crocodile Oily this story, a small water dweller came up the riverbank with a message for the Crocodile: 'Your wife has starved herself to death.'

Poor Oily began to weep: 'Oh dear, oh dear, what will become of me? The proverb says a home without a mother or a wife is no place to live. It is better to leave it. Ruddy, my friend, forgive my sins against you. Now that she is gone, I will burn myself alive.'

Ruddy laughed and said, 'Come, come. You are just proving again that you are a henpecked fool. One should celebrate when a wife like yours dies. As the wise men say, an ever-nagging wife should be avoided at all costs.'

'But what am I to do?' cried the Crocodile. 'I have lost my wife and my friend – that's two disasters at once. But I suppose I should remember the wife who lost her husband and her greedy friend, and was left with only an empty stare.'

'How was that?' asked the Monkey, and the Crocodile told this story.

Aged Farmer's Young Wife

There was an old but well-to-do farmer who had a small farm where he lived with his much younger wife. The Wife was bored, discontented and always on the lookout for someone to befriend her. One day when she was in a nearby village, a small-time but very handsome conman noticed her and thought he would try his luck with her.

He approached her and said, 'This is love at first sight. Will you be mine?' The Wife recklessly decided to run off with him. 'My husband is very old and wealthy. Wait here for me and I will go collect some valuables and we will go to some other village and live happily.'

The young rogue waited and the Wife returned with a large portion of her husband's money and valuables. Together, they started on their journey. After a while, they had to cross a river. Immediately the young man, who was a criminal, hatched a plan to rob the woman and run.

'The water in the river is deep and the current here is quite strong,' he told her. 'Perhaps I should go first with our belongings, leave them on the opposite bank and return to carry you across.' The besotted woman did what he asked her to do. So the rogue gathered his loot and swam across the river, never to return.

Eventually, the farmer's wife realized what had happened. Dejected, she sat and stared at the river. A female jackal came by with a chunk of raw meat in her mouth and saw a big fish leap out of the river and land on the bank. The jackal dropped the meat and sprang for the fish but missed. The fish wiggled back into the water and swam away. While the jackal was watching the fish, a vulture swooped down from the sky above, snatched the meat and flew away.

The woman smiled and mocked the jackal, 'So what do you wish for now that you have lost both meat and fish?'

The she-jackal replied, 'You are at least twice as clever as I am, yet all you have is an empty stare, having lost both husband and lover!'

While Oily was telling the story, yet another water dweller brought a message for Oily: 'Your home has been taken over by a very big crocodile.'

Hearing this, the Crocodile said, 'A strong stranger has taken over my house, my friend is mad at me and my wife is dead. Bad things don't happen one at a time. What shall I do? How shall I take back my house? Please, Ruddy, advise me.'

But the Monkey retorted 'You ungrateful fool! I have told you to go away. Why pursue me? Why should I give you good advice? *One should only give good advice to people best able to use it.* Remember the foolish monkey who destroyed the sparrow's cosy nest.'

'How was that?' asked the Crocodile, and the Monkey told this story.

Meddling Sparrow-hen

A Sparrow and his wife had built their cosy little nest on a branch of a tree. Underneath it, in the middle of winter, a Monkey took shelter. He had been caught in a

hailstorm and was wet and shivering. His teeth chattered and his hands and feet were numb.

The Sparrow-hen saw his miserable plight and said, 'You have hands and feet like a man's, so why don't you build a house for yourself, you fool!'

The Monkey was irritated and thought to himself, 'Everyone thinks they know best.' To the Sparrow-hen he said, 'Miss Smarty-pants! Hush up or I will spoil your party.' But the interfering Sparrow-hen continued to give him advice on how to build a house even when the Monkey had clearly told her to leave him alone. Eventually he got so mad that he shook the branch she lived on and destroyed her nest.

Having heard the story, the Crocodile still persisted.

'Oh my friend, I know I wronged you,' he said. 'But we were good friends once, so for old times' sake, please advise me.'

'I will not tell you to do one thing,' said Ruddy. 'You took your wife's advice and took me on your back under false pretences to my death. Even if you loved your wife, why hurt your friends and relatives because she asked you to?'

Oily still continued, 'I beg you to forgive me. You know men who give wise advice don't ever suffer here or hereafter.'

'Oh, all right,' said Ruddy at last. 'You had better go and fight the person who has taken over your home, for *it is said that one should be humble before the noble, use intrigue against heroes, give petty bribes to lackeys, but fight it out with equals.*'

'Tell me the tale,' begged the Crocodile, and the Monkey told this story.

How the Wily Jackal Ate the Elephant

A very clever jackal named Wily lived by his wits in a dense forest. One day he found an elephant that had died the same day of natural causes. The Jackal tried to bite through the thick hide to get at the meat but could not do so.

Just then, a Lion wandered into the copse where the elephant lay. Quickly, Wily bowed low to the ground and said, 'O King, I have been standing guard over your elephant. Please eat as much as you desire.'

'I never eat what I have not killed myself,' replied the Lion. 'I give the elephant to you.' And he left.

As soon as the Lion had gone, a Tiger appeared. Smart Wily figured he needed a different strategy. Being humble had worked with the Lion, but this time trickery would probably work better.

'O Sir, please beware,' he told the Tiger. 'This elephant was killed just now by a Lion. He left me to keep guard

and has gone to bathe in the river before having his meal. He did say before he left that if a tiger came by, I was to go at once to warn him for he intends to kill all tigers in this forest as revenge for the one tiger who stole his previous kill, giving him only the leavings.'

The Tiger fled for his life.

No sooner had the Tiger left than the Leopard arrived. Wily greeted him as a friend. 'I haven't seen you in ages. You are a welcome guest. Please help yourself to the elephant just killed by the Lion. I am appointed to guard it, but the Lion won't be back for a while. As my guest, help yourself and if I signal that the Lion is near, then run.'

The Leopard was hesitant, but Wily persuaded him to have a bite. Once the Leopard had made a deep cut in the elephant hide with his powerful fangs, the jackal gave the signal and the Leopard ran away.

When, finally, Wily was about to feast on the elephant, another jackal arrived. Wily recalled the maxim: *Bow to your superior, be devious facing the valiant, give bribes to the lower classes, confront your equals.* Wily rushed menacingly at the other jackal and easily killed him. Then he sat down and ate the elephant in comfort.

'So my advice is go and fight with the other crocodile,' said Ruddy. 'You are equals. If you don't, he will destroy you eventually. Remember, even if you leave and go to foreign lands, your kind there will still be a problem.'

'How so?' asked the Crocodile, and the Monkey told this story. ✐

Dog Who Went Abroad

A dog named Curly lived comfortably in a small town until a famine occurred. All the dogs and other domestic animals went hungry for days and weeks and months. Many, including Curly, became thin and weak, and the others starved to death. Curly decided to leave and go away to a city he had heard about.

Once he arrived in the foreign city, he met a generous lady who invited him to her house. He began going there regularly, was fed well and put on weight. But every time he left her door, he was surrounded by local dogs, powerful and proud, who often encircled him menacingly and sometimes attacked him. Eventually he got fed up with his situation and returned home.

His kinsman and friends who had survived the famine came running to greet him and ask him lots of questions. They were full of curiosity about his experiences abroad. So Curly recounted it in brief for them: 'There was plenty of good food, but only one thing was wrong. My own kind hated my guts for joining them there.'

After listening to his friend's advice, Oily the Crocodile decided to go home to oust the stranger who had taken over his house. He faced and fought him with courage and was victorious. ✍

Four Fortune Hunters

❧ Book Five ❧

About this Book

Book Five, here titled 'Four Fortune Hunters', is about drawing the wrong conclusions, and coming to hasty and devastating judgment as a result of misreading another creature's situation. It is also about abject poverty, and its consequences: the very worth of virtue, bravery, even learning, dims with poverty and people go to great lengths to escape it. But good or evil comes to good or bad people as Fate wills it and hoping against hope is an indulgence. One could say the book celebrates the crucial role of common sense triumphing over pretentious learning, self-importance and outrageous ambition. The greatest curse is that most dangerous ambition – greed.

After two initial *stand-alone* stories that highlight greed, the *frame* story becomes clear: it concerns four friends who decide to go abroad to lessen their poverty and make their fortune. While a Master-Magician gives each of them a magic quill to help them on their quest, only well-considered action pays dividends and disregarding a friend's advice turns out to be a disaster for one of the fortune seekers.

Gold-Finder reprimanding his friend, Wheel-Bearer (who ignored his advice and is left trapped in lifelong suffering), and the Wheel-Bearer's defence of his action are illustrated through the *nesting* stories. These, mostly single stand-alone stories, are separated in this book from the main one in a simple way: the pages with white background contain the nesting stories. This allows readers to choose whether they want to read them separately. The frame story of the fortune-hunting friends continues on the coloured pages and can be read without interruption of the nesting stories. The book can be read in its entirety to experience the original design of this book of stories. ✐

Four Fortune Hunters

Stories	Told By	To
• Greedy Barber	Sharma, Teacher	Three Princes
• Loyal Mongoose	Judge	Merchant
• Four Fortune Hunters	Brahmin's Wife	Brahmin
• A Dead Lion Lives Again	Gold-Finder	Wheel-Bearer
• Hundred-Wit, Thousand-Wit and Single-Wit	Wheel-Bearer	Gold-Finder
• Singing Donkey	Gold-Finder	Wheel-Bearer
• Simple Weaver	Wheel-Bearer	Gold-Finder
• Daydreaming Brahmin	Wheel-Bearer	Gold-Finder
• Avenging Chief-Monkey	Gold-Finder	Wheel-Bearer
• Credulous Demon	Gold-Finder	Wheel-Bearer
• Three-breasted Princess	Wheel-Bearer	Gold-Finder
• Inquiring Brahmin	Chamberlain	King

The fifth set of teaching tales Sharma told was:
Four Fortune Hunters.
    Sharma began:

'Never even think of actions
Ill-considered, consequential,
Disapproved, or done in haste;
Mind the tale of the Barber.'

    'How come?' asked the three Princes, and Sharma
told this story. ✑

Greedy Barber

There was an honest merchant who, as bad luck would have it, lost his fortune. He had lived his life in pursuit of happiness with both goodness and money, but once he became poor, he suffered every humiliation until he could stand it no longer. He reflected *how good character, good conduct and good sense become worthless when poverty crushes a man*. In his despair he decided that life was not worth living, so he would starve himself to death.

Having made up his mind, he went to bed. He slept and dreamt that he saw a Monk made of money and the Monk said to him, 'Do not lose hope. I am the wealth earned by your ancestors. I will appear again tomorrow morning. The minute you see me, you must club me on the head and my form will turn into pure gold.'

The next morning, without having any breakfast, the Merchant wondered whether the dream of the Monk would come true. *After all, not all dreams come true.*

*People who are sick, grieving, drunk or worried, all dream,
but their dreams don't come true.*

Meanwhile, the Merchant's wife had made an
appointment for that morning with a Barber to come
to the house to give her a manicure and her husband a
shave. The Barber duly arrived and began to give the wife
the manicure.

Just then the Monk appeared and the Merchant did
what he had been told to do in his dream the night before.
He picked up a club and hit the Monk on the head. The
Monk collapsed to the floor and turned into a pile of pure
gold. The Merchant was astonished and delighted, and
hid the treasure well out of sight.

However, the Barber had seen everything. When
he was leaving, the Merchant gave him a big tip and
asked him not to mention what he had seen to anybody.
The Barber agreed, but when he got home he thought
that he too could become rich, in fact, richer than the
Merchant. He decided to club all the monks he could
lure to his home.

The Barber knew of a seminary nearby where young
men went to study to become monks. So he plotted to
get all the young men who had already qualified to be
monks to come to his house under the false impression
that he was a pious man and needed their help. He told
the monks that he had some valuable manuscripts that
needed to be copied and that he would pay them well.
The young monks often earned money for the seminary

by acting as scribes to the outside world, so many agreed to come to the Barber's house.

When they arrived at the Barber's house, he clubbed all of them on the head. None of them turned into gold. The cries of the wounded were heard by neighbours and other villagers, and soon soldiers arrived to arrest the Barber and take him to court.

When questioned about his crimes by the Judge, the Barber wanted to know why the Merchant had not been arrested too. The Judge heard the Barber explain what had happened at the Merchant's house and sent for him. The honest Merchant described what had happened to him. The Judge punished the Barber for he had heedlessly killed many monks and injured others.

'*No person,*' the Judge said '*should take action without properly seeing, understanding, hearing or examining the matter at hand. Only well-considered action should ever be undertaken.* Otherwise, like the lady and the mongoose, you will be filled with remorse all your life.'

'How is that?' asked the Merchant, and the Judge told this story.

Loyal Mongoose

A Brahmin and his wife lived in a small town with their toddler son and a pet Mongoose whom the wife had reared as if he were her second son. But deep inside, she didn't really trust the Mongoose. She thought that the Mongoose might hurt her son.

One day, she said to her husband as she tucked her son in bed for a nap, 'Please do not leave our son alone. I have to go to get some water from the village well.'

However, he did not pay any attention to his wife's request and left soon after to beg for some food for the family. He was not long gone when a big black snake came into the house and slithered into the baby's room. Being a natural enemy of the snake, the Mongoose saw him and immediately sprang at the snake to protect the baby's life. He fought with the snake and eventually killed him. Then, very pleased with himself, and with the snake's blood still all over his face, he went off to meet the Wife on her way home.

But when she saw the Mongoose with blood on his mouth, she jumped to the conclusion that he had killed her son. So, without thinking, she hit the Mongoose on the head with her water-jar and killed him instantly.

When she got home, she saw her baby was safe and still sound asleep in his crib while the dead snake's mauled and bloody corpse lay nearby. She finally realized what had happened. Overwhelmed that she had killed the saviour of her child, she began to weep. When the Brahmin returned home, she blamed him bitterly for not doing what she had told him to do, thereby causing her second son's death: 'You could have waited to eat,' she said. 'Remember the greedy fellow who had a whirling wheel on his head?'

'Who was that?' asked the Brahmin, and his wife told him this story.

Four Fortune Hunters

There were four fast friends, all Brahmin men, all very poor, who decided to get together to discuss their common plight. *They all knew that poverty ruined everything in life. Charm, courage, wit and good looks are useless without money. Friends, relatives, even children keep their distance; the worth of virtue, bravery and even learning dims with poverty.* So the friends decided to try and make money, no matter the cost. They thought it was better to be dead than penniless.

The four friends figured that *there were six ways of making money: begging, serving the upper classes, working on a farm, teaching in a school, trading, or becoming moneylenders.* Only trading seemed to have no downside, allowed making large amounts of money, and therefore was most acceptable to them.

However, even trade that leads to profit can have seven temptations or related challenges: using false weights and balances, hiking up prices, opening a pawn shop and lending money against items kept as security, somehow attracting repeat customers, selling livestock or luxuries, and foreign trade. Again, they found problems with each, eventually decided upon foreign trade and therefore needed to travel to foreign lands.

After they had been travelling a while, they met a Master-Magician and went with him to his monastery. He asked them where they were from, where they were going and why.

The friends replied, 'We are pilgrims seeking powers of magic ourselves. We are very poor and have decided to search for riches, or die. They say that great effort pays off. Do, please, show us a way of making money, no matter what we have to do to get it.'

So the Master-Magician made four magic quills and gave one to each of the four friends, saying, 'Wherever the quill drops, the owner will find treasure.'

The first quill fell on the way and the owner found that the soil covered a hoard of copper. He told his friends, 'We can share this wealth. You can each take all you want.' But the others did not see the value in doing so. They felt they would find silver ahead, more valuable than copper. In fact, they encouraged him to leave his find and go on with them, but he declined. He took his copper and turned back, and the other three friends continued their search.

Further along, the second quill dropped and the owner found a trove of silver. He was delighted and told his friends, 'We can share. You can each take all you want.' But the others were sure there would be gold ahead and urged him to continue along with them. But he declined, took his silver and turned back.

The third quill dropped and the owner found a cache of pure gold. He was thrilled and said to his friend, 'We can share. You can take all the gold you want,' but the other said, 'You are foolish. We will find gems next, so come ahead with me.'

However, Gold-Finder declined. 'I will wait here for you. You are being greedy and should not go off alone.' But the fourth friend left and went ahead.

He travelled a long time, very hungry and thirsty. He finally saw a man on a whirling platform with a rotating wheel on his head. The Wheel-Bearer was clearly in pain and drops of blood dripped down his face.

The last friend asked him, 'Why are you standing there with a wheel turning on your head? Anyway, tell me where I can find water. I am dying of thirst.'

The minute the fourth friend said this, the wheel left the other man's head and settled on his head!

'What is this?' the friend asked. 'This wheel hurts. When will I be free of it?'

The other man replied, 'When someone holds a magic quill like yours and speaks as you just did – only then will the wheel leave you.'

The friend asked, 'How long were you here?'

'Centuries!' came the answer. 'The wheel is the result of a curse by the Master-Magician to keep greedy people from reaching or taking the last treasures that belong to him.' And he vanished.

Eventually, Gold-Finder came looking for the last friend. He heard his sad tale and scolded him: 'You didn't listen to me. Remember the scholars without common sense who made a dead lion come alive, and got killed."

'How was that?' asked the poor Wheel-Bearer, and the Gold-Finder told this story.

A Dead Lion Lives Again

There were four Brahmins who were close friends. They had grown up in the same village. Three were true scholars and had achieved high honours for their knowledge of all the arts and sciences. The fourth had, however, taken a different road. He was a simple man of sense, good common sense, and had refused to follow in the footsteps of his friends.

One day the friends were chatting and one of them said, 'What is the worth of all this learning we have acquired? We should travel, win the patronage of kings and get rich.' So they left their village for foreign lands.

They had not gone far when one of them said, 'We won't *all* win acclaim. One of us has no scholarship at all. So he will not be sharing our wealth. Maybe he should turn back?'

The second friend agreed, but the third friend said, 'No, this is no way to behave towards our childhood friend. Please let him come with us and share any wealth we earn.' So the four friends continued their quest.

When they were passing through a jungle, they came upon the bones of a dead lion.

One scholar said, 'Hey, why don't we test our knowledge on this dead creature? I can set all the bones together to make a proper skeleton.'

The second scholar rushed to say, 'I know how to get together flesh, blood and skin.'

'Well, I know how to give it life,' said the third scholar.

So the first and second scholars set about and performed their tasks successfully. But, as the third scholar was about to breathe life into the dead lion, the fourth friend, the sensible one, stopped him, and said, 'Don't do it. If you bring a lion to life, he will kill us all.'

The third scholar replied, 'You really are a fool. You do not understand our level of scholarship!'

The man of sense responded, 'All right, if you are going ahead, please wait till I climb up that tall tree.'

When the third scholar breathed life into the lion, he killed and ate all three scholars, and then wandered off to find some water. The man of sense climbed down carefully and returned home.

The Wheel-Bearer, however, did not agree with the lesson of the story.

He said, 'Not all men of great sense do well. Sometimes those with very little sense can, with a little bit of luck, do very well. Remember the proverb: *Hundred-Wit was on the head, Thousand-Wit hung from the shoulder, but I, Single-Wit, am alive in clean, clear water.*'

'What do you mean?' asked the Gold-Finder, and the Wheel-Bearer told this story.

Hundred-Wit, Thousand-Wit and Single-Wit

Two fish, who were very smart, lived together in a large pond. They were nicknamed Hundred-Wit and Thousand-Wit because they were very clever. They made friends with a frog called Single-Wit who was thought to be simple. Despite their differences, the three friends often had good conversations together, hanging out at the edge of the pond.

One day they overheard some fishermen who were standing at the water's edge, surveying the pond. 'Look,' said one, 'this pond is teeming with fish. Let us come here early tomorrow morning with our rods and nets, and get a good catch.'

The three friends were upset. The Frog was the first to speak. 'What should we do? Stay or flee?'

Thousand-Wit laughed and said, 'I don't think the fishermen will show up, but even if they do, I can outsmart them. So I shall stay.'

Hundred-Wit agreed with his fish friend. 'Why should we leave home? *The wise always find a way out of problems.*'

But the Frog said, 'I am Single-Wit and I am telling myself to flee.' So, later that night, the Frog and his wife fled to another smaller lake nearby.

Late next morning, what did they see but two fishermen going home with their catch of the day!

'See,' said the Frog to his wife, 'one carries Hundred-Wit on his head, the other hangs Thousand-Wit on his shoulder, but I, Single-Wit, am alive with you in clear, clean water.'

The Gold-Finder heard the Wheel-Bearer's story but continued, 'Yet *one should not always disregard a friend's advice.* I told you to stop and share my gold with me. You were too proud of your smartness and too greedy. You should have remembered the singing donkey.'

'What do you mean?' asked the Wheel-Bearer and the Gold-Finder told this story. ✆

Singing Donkey

There was a donkey named Headstrong who made friends with a Jackal. The Donkey worked for his master who was a laundryman, but at night he was allowed to roam free. The Jackal and Donkey would raid different fields at night, eat their fill and return to their own homes early, before the watchful farmers were up.

One night, the Donkey, standing in a cucumber field, said to his fellow thief, the Jackal, 'The night is so beautiful. I feel like singing.'

The Jackal was astonished and advised the Donkey, 'Please don't sing. We are thieves. Singing will alert the farmers and you will come to grief.'

'You really are not a music lover – haven't you heard of the magic of music?' the Donkey responded.

'I have,' said the Jackal, 'but your braying is harsh and will carry across the fields. Why do something that can only harm you?'

'So you think I cannot sing!' said the obstinate Donkey. 'I am well conversant with musicology. How can you stop me?'

'OK,' said the Jackal, 'sing your heart out. I will stay at the edge of the field as a lookout for the farmers.'

The Donkey began to sing, and the farmers came running. They beat him, put a millstone round his neck and went home.

The Donkey ran away and never came back to the fields.

The Jackal said to himself with a smile: 'You sang so well and now you have a medal for it round your neck!'

Gold-Finder again reminded the Wheel-Bearer, 'You should have listened to me.'

'Yes, you are right,' said the Wheel-Bearer finally. '*Without wit, one should at least listen to a friend*. I should have remembered the simple weaver who came to a fatal end.'

'How was that?' asked the Gold-Finder, and the Wheel-Bearer told this story. ✒

Simple Weaver

A Weaver lived with his wife in a small town in the east of the country. He worked hard and made a modest living. One day, as luck would have it, all the pegs in his loom broke. So he took his axe and went into the nearby forest to look for a suitable tree to cut down and use the wood to make new pegs.

After spending quite some time searching for just the right tree, the Weaver came upon one that would give him plenty of new weaving pegs and tools. So he lifted his axe to cut it down. Just then he heard a voice say, 'Please spare my tree. I have lived here happily for a very long time.'

'But,' replied the Weaver, 'I have no choice. I am so sorry to do this. However, this is the right tree from which to make my pegs or without them my family will starve. Couldn't you please move to another tree?'

The voice above, which belonged to a tree fairy, then said, 'You are a good man. I will grant you one wish for anything you like if you do not cut down my tree.'

The Weaver was very pleased and replied that he needed to discuss this with his wife and a friend before choosing the wish, so he would return the next day.

On his way back to town, he met his friend, explained what he needed and requested his advice on what he should ask for. His friend said promptly, 'Ask for a kingdom. Then you can be king and I can be your prime minister, and we can live happily ever after.'

'That sounds like a very good idea, but I need to check it out with my wife.'

'Oh, don't do that,' said his friend. '*Wives should be loved and showered with gifts, but one should never seek their advice.*'

'You may be right,' said the Weaver, 'but I will consult her. She is a good wife.'

The Weaver then went home and told his wife what had happened, what the fairy had offered and what his friend had advised. 'Oh, your friend is a barber!' she said. 'What sense does a barber have? Being a king and having to rule brings not only trouble but also the danger of being overthrown. Don't listen to your friend.'

'Then what should I ask for?' asked the Weaver. To which the wife replied, 'You make a good but modest living. Why not ask the fairy to double it by giving you an extra pair of hands and a second head? That should make us comfortable.'

So the simple Weaver went to the fairy and asked for a second pair of hands and a second head, which she readily gave him.

However, on the way, the townspeople saw him and they thought he was some kind of demon. They were so frightened of him that they killed him.

'Yes,' said the Wheel-Bearer, '*any man becomes ridiculous when seduced by absurd dreams. That is why they warn against having any grand hopes,* or you will become all white like the father of Monsoon.'

'How was that?' asked the Gold-Finder, and the Wheel-Bearer told this story. ✍

Daydreaming Brahmin

There lived a poor Brahmin who made his living by begging. Once he was given a good amount of barley meal. After eating some, he saved the rest in an earthen pot and hung it above his bed. As he was about to fall asleep, he started to daydream:

There would be a famine and his store of barley meal would fetch a hundred rupees. With that money he would buy a pair of goats who would have many young goats and within a couple of years he would have a herd, which he could sell. Then he would buy a pair of cows who would have many calves. These he would sell to buy buffaloes. Eventually he would buy and breed horses that would sell for gold. With the gold he would buy a great mansion and then a rich man would offer his daughter to him and she would bring a large dowry.

'Then we will have a son,' he continued to dream, 'whom I will name Moonson. When my son is old enough he will want to sit on my knee as often as possible. But I will be busy and sometimes I will ask my wife to take him

and if she doesn't do it right away, I will be very angry with her.'

As the Brahmin was daydreaming of his anger, he actually let fly a high kick that shattered the barley meal pot above his bed and made him white from head to toe.

'You are right,' said the Gold-Finder. 'Greedy people do not pay attention to the results of what they do, just like King Star.'

'What happened to King Star?' asked the Wheel-Bearer, and the Gold-Finder told this story. ✍

Avenging Chief-Monkey

There was a small city-state ruled by a King named Star. He was very indulgent and kept a pack of monkeys and a herd of rams for his son's amusement. The Prince enjoyed getting the rams to fight each other and having the monkeys perform all kinds of tricks. He had his servants feed the animals well. But the rams were bold and always hungry and went into the royal kitchens quite often to get whatever was available to eat. The cooks were very unhappy and fought the rams off as best they could to keep the palace dinners from being spoiled.

The Chief-Monkey saw the problems between the cooks and the rams. He worried that there would be a fight and the cooks would one day hit the rams with a burning log and set fire to them. If the burning rams went into the stables next door, the hay there would quickly catch fire and the horses would be harmed. If that happened, the monkeys would be in trouble because veterinarians believed that the only way to heal a horse that has been burned is by using monkey fat for balm. That would lead to the killing of monkeys.

The Chief-Monkey was known for his foresight and knew the situation was a tragedy waiting to happen. So he went to his troop of monkeys, explained what he feared, and suggested they leave and go to the woods for safety. 'One should flee senseless quarrels,' he thought. But the young monkeys didn't want to give up their easy life. They simply ignored the Chief-Monkey's warning as undue worrying by an old-timer. So the Chief-Monkey left alone for the woods. He could not bear to wait and witness the destruction of his troop.

A day later the Chief-Monkey's fears came true. The rams came into the kitchen, the angry cook threw a burning log at them, the coat of two of the rams caught fire, the rams ran to the stables, set the store of hay ablaze and the King's horses were badly burned. The King had not thought through the consequences of his actions and ordered the whole troop of monkeys to be killed so the animal doctor would have the monkey fat he needed to heal the King's horses.

As it happened, the Chief-Monkey had come to the edge of a pond when he left the palace, and was about to enter it to quench his thirst, when he noticed that there were many footprints going to the pond but none coming back. So he decided to be cautious and drank the water standing on the shore, using the hollow stem of the lotus flower as a straw.

Now there was a Monster who lived in the pond and ate every creature that entered the deep water. He had noticed the Chief-Monkey's caution and said, 'Well done. Your caution has helped you escape from me. I eat everyone who jumps into the pond. I have taken a liking to you. Is there anything I can do for you?'

By this time the Chief-Monkey had heard the news of the slaughter of his clan. He could not let it go and was set on revenge. So he immediately asked the Monster, 'If I lured people to enter your pond, how many can you eat?'

'As many as you bring me and more!' replied the Monster.

'I live in deadly hatred of King Star,' explained the Chief-Monkey. 'I will try and awaken his greed by a believable story, but to be successful I need you to lend me your necklace of rubies.' The Monster understood the Chief-Monkey's plan and decided to befriend him by loaning him his ruby necklace.

The Chief-Monkey returned to the palace wearing the ruby necklace and told King Star a false story about how he got it from the pond.

The King and his people all wanted to go to the pond so they could get similar necklaces. When the Chief-Monkey saw they were all hooked, he led a procession to the pond but insisted that he and the King be the last ones to jump into the pond. Thus all the King's subjects leapt in and all were eaten up by the Monster.

Then the Chief-Monkey climbed up a high tree, and from his safe position shouted down to the King, 'You killed my entire clan and now I have killed all your subjects. I didn't kill you because you are my king, but I see no wrong in repaying evil with evil.'

Having told the story, Gold-Finder told the Wheel-Bearer, 'Please bid me goodbye. I want to go home now.'

'But you can't leave me in this plight!' replied the Wheel-Bearer. 'Deserting a friend will lead you straight to hell.'

'That is true,' said the Gold-Finder, 'but only if I can really help and the friend is in a situation from which he can be rescued. The more I look at you, the more I am reminded that if I don't leave right now I will also be caught in Twilight's cruel grip.'

'What are you saying?' asked the Wheel-Bearer, and Gold-Finder told this story. ✑

Credulous Demon

Once there lived a King who had a very beautiful daughter named Pearl. She lived with her parents in the palace and had a magic circle around her to prevent her from being harmed. However, there was a Demon who troubled her every night and the poor Princess Pearl felt extreme fear, and trembled and tossed and turned feverishly. She couldn't get rid of the unseen Demon and he couldn't take her away because of the magic circle.

One night, the Demon showed himself to the Princess and she, at once, pointed him out to her maid saying, 'Look, there is the Demon who comes with Twilight to torment me. Is there any way to keep him away?'

The Demon misunderstood her words. He thought he was not the only demon who visited her. He thought there was another demon called Twilight, who also came every night but could not carry her away either.

'I had better take the form of a horse,' the Demon thought, 'and find out what form the other demon takes and what power he has.' So the Demon turned himself

into a horse and stood in the King's stables, on the lookout for his rival.

As it happened, a horse thief came into the stables and chose the Demon-horse to steal. He saddled him, put the bit in his mouth and kicked him with his spurs. The Demon-horse got worried that the horse thief was his rival and took off at a brisk pace.

When the horse thief struck him with a whip, the Demon-horse galloped away at a speed the horse thief had never before seen. As the rider tried to control the Demon-horse, it galloped even faster. Realizing that something was very wrong, the horse thief steered the horse under a banyan tree, and jumped up and caught a branch while the Demon-horse kept running on.

Once separated, they were both relieved. But then a monkey butted in and called out to the Demon-horse, 'Why run from an imaginary danger? Your rider is just a man. Kill him.' So the Demon changed back into his usual form and came back to the banyan tree. But the thief who was sitting on the branch below the monkey grabbed the monkey's tail and starting biting and chewing it very hard. The monkey felt trapped and dared not move or say anything.

The Demon looked at him and said, 'Judging by your face, dear monkey, you have been caught in Twilight's cruel grip.' And so the Demon went away.

Once the story came to an end, Gold-Finder said again, 'Bid me farewell. I want to go home. You may stay here and suffer the consequences of your greed and of ignoring a a friend's advice.'

'That is not so,' said the Wheel-Bearer. 'Good or evil comes to good or bad people as fate wills it. As the old tale goes, whether a hunchback, a blind man, or a princess with three breasts, fortune favours whom it wills.'

'How so?' asked the Gold-Finder, and the Wheel-Bearer told this story.

Three-breasted Princess

In a city in the centre of the North country, lived a King whose Queen gave birth to a three-breasted girl. As soon as he heard the news, the King summoned the Chamberlain and ordered that the girl be taken from the palace and left in the forest so that no one would ever know about her.

The Chamberlain answered that the King should consult holy Brahmins, so that any action he undertook under the sad circumstances would not offend any laws, human or divine. 'For the proverb says a prudent man always enquires into things beyond his understanding, like the Brahmin caught by a fiend but freed again,' said the Chamberlain.

'How was that?' asked the King, and his Chamberlain told this story.

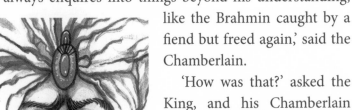

Inquiring Brahmin

In a forest there lived a cruel fiend who treated everyone who wandered into his territory very badly. One day a Brahmin was crossing the forest. The Fiend caught him, climbed on to the Brahmin's shoulders, and made him carry him wherever he wanted to go in the jungle.

Since the Fiend was sitting on the Brahmin's shoulders with his legs dangling in front, the Brahmin noticed that he had soft supple feet with no corns or callouses. So the Brahmin asked the Fiend, 'Please, Sir, why are your feet so tender?' and the Fiend replied, 'I am under a vow never to touch the ground with my bare feet.'

Soon they came to a pond where the Fiend wanted a wash, so he told the Brahmin to stand at the edge of the pond and not stir until he had finished bathing. The Brahmin realized that if he waited, the Fiend would eat him, but if he ran away, the Fiend would probably not come after him immediately because of his vow. And so the Brahmin quickly escaped.

*

After listening to the story, the King discussed the fate of the Princess with the palace Brahmins. They advised that the King should not look upon his daughter and that he should make a proclamation that if any man would marry the Princess, he would give the man a hundred thousand pieces of gold, but the couple would have to live in a foreign land.

Time passed but no one asked for the hand of the Princess. Then a young blind man in a nearby city, who had a hunchback servant to help him manage daily chores, remembered the proclamation and decided to offer to marry the Princess. Shortly thereafter, the Blind Man married the three-breasted Princess and with the Hunchback, the threesome left for foreign lands with their riches.

They found a comfortable house and lived together for some months in harmony. But the Hunchback did all the work while the Blind Man dozed all day. After some more time passed, the Princess began to dislike her husband so much that she asked the Hunchback to find her some poison so she could kill her husband.

The Hunchback found the body of a deadly snake that the Princess cut up and seasoned to make a delicious smelling stew. As it was simmering on the stove, the Princess asked her husband to stir it from time to time, for she had to go shopping and the Hunchback was busy in the fields. The husband began his task in the kitchen.

As the steam from the poison stew rose and stung his eyes, the Blind Man suddenly noticed that he could see some light. After a while, his vision cleared completely and he could see! He was no longer completely blind! Then he looked in the pot to see what could have caused the miracle. He saw pieces of the venomous snake in the bottom of the pot and realized what was going on. This was a plot to kill him! But he kept his cool and when the Princess and the Hunchback returned he did not let on that he could see and watched them very closely.

He came to the conclusion that his long-time companion, the Hunchback, was at fault. He picked the Hunchback up by his feet and hurled him at the Princess. The result was totally unexpected: the blow shoved the Princess' third breast back into her body and the curved back of the Hunchback straightened as his legs were pulled hard!

When the Wheel-Bearer finished the story, the Gold-Finder said, 'You are right. Good things can happen, but only if fate wills it. I hope things work out for you. Goodbye.'

And the Gold-Finder left. 🖂

'Now… we come to the End,' announced Sharma.

'You mean you are not going to tell us any more stories?' asked the three Princes.

'That is correct,' said Sharma. 'From now on, you will be on your own.

'Remember…

'Should you choose
To learn as taught,
You will never lose
No matter what.'

Acknowledgements

As I have noted elsewhere, the *Panchatantra* stories (literally Five Books) have been part of India's oral and scholarly tradition for at least 2,000 years or more. They have been told and retold all over the world and have influenced many literary genres, particularly those containing animal characters and 'nesting stories', i.e., one story in another story in another story. Sometime towards the end of the twelfth century, the seminal version of the *Panchatantra* was written by Vishnu Sharma in Sanskrit and has formed the best-known rendition ever since. It comprises a vast array of folk wisdom interspersed with 85 stories that collectively serve as a guidebook of sorts on how to live a wise and good life. Many translations of the text are available in English and some selected stories have been published for young children. However, the entire collection has never been adapted for casual readers, whether teenagers or adults.

My goal is to make the core of the *Panchatantra* easily accessible to the English speaking world. I have delved deeply into three authoritative, literal translations of the complete text of the *Panchatantra* from the original Sanskrit by three eminent scholars: Arthur W. Rider (1925), Chandra Rajan (1993) and Patrick Olivelle (1997). Their work represents the best of what serious academics have to offer. I am clearly indebted to them.

Nevertheless, the original in its entirety remains rather difficult to register and enjoy for non-academics. I have used their translations to understand and stay as close to the original of the *Panchatantra* as possible. Beyond that, the way I have organized the five books for a lay audience, the telling of the stories, the language used, and the summary of the wisdom highlighted by the stories, are entirely mine.

I have read and re-read the stories in various forms over the last 50 years. I wish I had a way of publicly thanking all the authors I have read on the subject of the *Panchatantra*. Suffice it to say, their work taught me that these ancient stories are the essence of Indian wisdom and values that deserve a wide international audience.

Throughout this venture, my husband Michael has been my strongest backer, my sharpest critic, my meticulous editor, and my most long-suffering love. I cannot thank him enough. I also owe thanks to my children, Kieran and Sean, who never failed to point out that my stories were not PC enough for children, and to my friends, Roland, Judy and Jon, who did not hesitate to point out that my storytelling was too confusing even for adults. I hope they will see that I took their judgments seriously.

I hope that my enthusiasm for these stories is catching. Cheers.

Narindar Uberoi Kelly, 2017